Lifeblood:

INHERITANCE LOST

Lifeblood:

INHERITANCE LOST

ELIZABETH ANNE GREY

Lifeblood: Inheritance Lost

Elizabeth Anne Grey

This book is a work of fiction. All names, places, characters, and events are products of the author's imagination and are fictitious. Any similarities to actual events, places, people, living or dead, is coincidental.

Cover design by Enchanted Ink Publishing

Dark Citrine LLC

WWW.DARKCITRINE.NET

PO BOX 2455
Mount Vernon, WA 98273

First Edition:

ISBN: 978-1-7378365-0-6 (Hard Copy)
ISBN: 978-1-7378365-1-3 (Paperback)
ISBN: 978-1-7378365-2-0 (eBook)

Printed in the United States of America

Earl Edward Grey, thank you for being ever present even in your absence.

PROLOGUE

"WAIT FOR ME!" Her breathing was rapid as she ran down the long road that seemed to lead nowhere. Her legs shook with each stride, and her mind raced, knowing she would never catch him. Then he stopped.

"Come on!" he called out to her. "I know you can run faster than that."

Alexis grimaced when she finally reached Sebastian, panting hard under the hot sun. "You have longer legs than I do."

Sebastian laughed. "Yeah right, that's why I beat you."

Alexis dropped her eyes, kicking a rock in her path.

"Hey, come on," he began. "I was only kidding. You're faster than any other girl I know."

"Really?" she asked, encouraged by the statement. "Is that why you give me a hard time?"

He stared at her for a moment before continuing down the long dirt road. She matched his pace, walking proudly beside him.

She was leaving tomorrow with her grandmother, and who knew when they would see each other again. They had known each other for years, it seemed, but what did he know? He was only eight years old, and she was six.

They were used to seeing each other every day, and now Alexis and her parents were moving away, all the way to Washington State. That was two whole states away from him. He couldn't understand why they were leaving. California was great. Sebastian's pace picked up. He looked up at the evening sky filled with color.

"Are you mad at me?" Trailing behind she ran to catch up with him.

"No, I'm not mad at you. I just don't know why you have to move so far away."

"Mom said Dad got a better job offer, and I guess it's a pretty big deal." She wasn't happy herself with her parents' decision.

They walked along in silence for some time until they came to the end of the road, admiring the sun dipping lower in the sky.

"Guess we should head back now," he announced.

"I guess so."

Alexis turned to walk back in the direction they came from when Sebastian grabbed her hand, pulling her closer to him. He stepped forward, and before she knew what was happening, he leaned down and pressed his lips against hers. She froze, her heart pounding. She closed her eyes, holding her breath and wondering how long it would last, and then the kiss ended.

She opened her eyes to find him staring at her, smiling. She managed a smile, and they walked hand in hand back towards Sebastian's house, enjoying the sounds of nature and the cars in the distance.

The next morning, Alexis sat in the front seat, waving to her parents and watching Sebastian, who was on the porch, head hung low. She was going to miss him, now more than ever. She just needed him to look up one last time before they drove away. He finally did. He waved and even managed a smile, but she could tell he was sad too.

"Well, kiddo," Gram began, "we're getting an early enough start, and if traffic isn't too bad, we can probably reach my house before midnight. How does that sound?"

"Late." Alexis looked past her grandmother, glancing one last time at the boy on the porch.

"Oh, I know you're going to miss it here, but there are a lot of exciting things waiting to be discovered in Washington, and your parents will be up in just a few days."

"Can we call them when we get there?"

"Since it's going to be late, we'll call them first thing in the morning. How does that sound?"

"Okay," Alexis replied, smiling at Gram.

Gram smiled, moving the car down the driveway. She reached for the volume on the radio, turning up a catchy tune she knew her granddaughter loved. Anything she could do to help lift her spirits. She knew Alexis was going to miss Sebastian, but she would be fine. It was just the initial good-bye that was difficult. Then again, who knew what the future would bring?

They stopped along the way for some lunch, took a few quick breaks here and there, and before they knew it, the lights of the Seattle skyline were filling the night sky. Gram pulled into the driveway, helping Alexis with all the bags she had packed. The rest of her things would be arriving in the next few days.

"Did you see the looks between Sebastian and Alexis last night?" Joanna asked her husband, a mischievous grin on her face.

"I sure did," Nathaniel replied, laughing.

"I wish we could tell them they won't be apart forever, that they are actually destined to be together."

"That would invite too many questions, don't you think?" he asked. "Alexis doesn't like to give up when she feels like she doesn't have all the answers."

"That's true," Joanna agreed, reaching out to tuck some stray hair behind his ear. "I think she gets it from me."

"Definitely," Nathaniel teased, proud of how inquisitive his daughter could be. He leaned over to kiss his wife.

"Dinner was great, thank you."

"You sure did eat a lot tonight," he announced. "Wait . . ."

Nathaniel turned, admiring his wife's beautiful face. Her long dark hair was pulled back in a ponytail, and her bright green eyes were shining with excitement. Her smile was undeniable.

"How do you think Alexis will take the news?"

"I think she's going to be extremely excited. You've seen her with little Maxi, haven't you?"

Nathaniel nodded. "It was funny to watch how protective Sebastian was of his little sister."

"I think he's going to grow into a fine young man," Joanna said.

"I think you're right. Do you want to catch a movie, make this a full date night?"

"That sounds great. I love you."

"I love you too." Nathaniel leaned over, kissing his wife again, enjoying the scent of her sun-kissed skin.

They stared at each other a moment longer before he reached to turn the ignition over. The car exploded, erupting into flames, debris flying everywhere. People came from every direction to see what had happened, while others ran to call for help.

A figure standing in the shadow of a nearby building watched from afar, delighted the task was done. Too bad he missed the little one, but soon . . .

CHAPTER 1

Seattle, 1982

SHE WAS BREATHLESS with anticipation, hanging on his every word. The room was dark except for a single light shining directly on him. It felt like they were the only two people in the lecture hall, although Alexis knew that was not the case. The buzz and chatter from the other students in her Art History class were gone now, replaced with the hypnotic sound of a voice that accelerated her heart and quieted her mind at the same time. Despite the fact that she was sitting fifteen feet away, in the second row, almost directly in front of the podium from world-renowned art collector, Aidan Drake, to Alexis his face seemed like it was only inches from her own. During the lecture, it felt like he was speaking directly to her, looking deep into her eyes, and she was captivated.

Applause brought her back to reality, and she blinked a few times, looking around at her fellow students as the lights came up, filling the room. She was confused. It seemed like the lecture had just started moments before. She shook her head, gathering her notes and books together to put into her bag, watching a few students approach Mr. Drake on stage at the podium. How could she not remember the lecture? She glanced at her watch, noting an hour had passed.

Standing, she ran her moist hands down the front of her new black jeans, smoothing the material. She smiled when she realized how sweaty they were. Why was she so nervous? She adjusted the hem of the emerald-green V-neck sweater she was wearing before pulling her tailored black leather coat on. Thankfully, she was still thinking clearly when she'd selected her outfit this morning; sophisticated and understated, two things she did not feel right now. Tossing her long dark hair over her shoulders before picking up her book bag, she walked quickly down the row to the empty aisle, turning towards the stage. She paused, watching him speak with another student, and as she approached she could hear questions being asked about his private collection and the rare pieces he had acquired from all over the world. Alexis had read articles in art magazines about Mr. Drake's private collection being worth millions and how generous he had been, having quite a few pieces on display in several galleries all over the country.

Ascending the stairs to the stage, she slowed her pace, waiting for the other students to walk away. She wanted to speak with him alone. As she approached the podium, Mr. Drake looked over, smiling at her as he gathered his books and lecture notes. He was wearing a black suit with a light gray turtleneck underneath. He was very handsome, probably in his forties, of average height, yet somehow his presence filled the stage. His dark hair was combed straight back, and his dark eyebrows stood out against his alabaster skin, accentuating his translucent blue eyes. He was clean-shaven with a strong jawline, which might have been intimidating for some, and his posture and build suggested he took care of himself.

"Mr. Drake, I was wondering if you had a moment. I had some questions I would like to ask you?" Warmth spread through her, and her heart pounded in her chest so hard, she knew he could hear it too.

He smiled. "Please, call me Aidan. It is Alexis, right? Alexis McBain?"

Her breath suddenly left her body, making it difficult to speak. "Yes, that's right. How did you know my name?"

He smiled, gesturing at the paper in his hand. "It's listed right here on the attendance sheet. You were sitting in the second row almost directly in front of me," he replied, pointing at the seating chart. "Alexis, right?"

"Yes, that's right. I'm so sorry," she gushed, feeling even more embarrassed than before. "I've just been following you for so long, I mean following your career. I guess I'm just a little overwhelmed actually meeting you, Mr. Drake, Aidan."

"That's okay." His smile widened. "What would you like to ask me?"

Alexis stared at him, finally finding her words. "I was wondering when the local gallery you've invested in will be reopening. I've heard you're going to have some of your private collection added. Is that correct?"

"It's actually opening this Saturday, and yes, I will have a few pieces from my private collection there," he replied. "Would you like to come to the opening?"

"That would be awesome! Oh, but I have plans, I'm sorry. It's my birthday. Well, actually today is my birthday, and my boyfriend will be taking me out to dinner Saturday night." She hated when she rambled.

He smiled. "Happy birthday. I could add your names to the list, and you could come after your dinner."

"Thank you very much. That's so generous of you, and I look forward to seeing your collection."

They continued talking about several art periods and artists, and Alexis was feeling more relaxed the longer the conversation went on. She had lost track of the time until Sebastian appeared by her side.

"Is everything okay?" Sebastian asked Alexis, looking at Aidan.

"Yes," she replied. "Oh, Sebastian, I'm sorry. I missed our lunch date. Mr. Drake, this is my boyfriend, Sebastian. Sebastian, this is Aidan Drake. We just got caught up talking about art periods and his collection, which will be on exhibit in the gallery when it reopens this Saturday. Aidan is adding our names to the list so we can stop by after dinner."

"It's nice to meet you, Mr. Drake," Sebastian said, extending his arm to shake hands.

"It's a pleasure meeting you as well," Aidan replied.

Sebastian couldn't help but notice a hardness about the man as the two shook hands. It was odd. His eyes were cold in comparison to the warm smile displayed on his face. Sebastian knew immediately something was off with this guy.

"Well, thank you again, I really enjoyed the lecture, and I look forward to the gallery opening," Alexis said.

"I will see both of you there." Aidan smiled at them, his eyes lingering on Alexis.

Alexis and Sebastian left the lecture hall, walking hand in hand through the corridor, the heels of her boots echoing off the walls of the building. It felt like Sebastian was pulling her along, his pace faster than usual, almost as if he couldn't put enough distance between them and Aidan.

"Hey, babe," Alexis said, tugging on his hand. "Is everything okay?"

Sebastian turned his athletic six-foot-two frame to study her beautiful face, a flush in her cheeks adding color to her usual porcelain complexion. He gently caressed her right cheek with his fingertips, looking deep into her eyes for a moment, his hazel-green eyes causing her heart to melt.

"I'm good. I just get a weird vibe from the guest lecturer."

"Aidan?"

"Yeah, Aidan. There's just something about him that seemed a bit . . . off."

"Well, maybe it's just because he's so worldly and charismatic," she stated, a mischievous grin on her face. She reached up with her right hand to run her fingers through his short dark brown hair, placing her hand on his chest.

"Funny girl." He pulled her in for a kiss. "You should be punished for that comment."

"Mm, later," she replied coyly, stepping back and enjoying the taste of his kiss on her lips. "I have another class to get to right now."

"Well then, I will have to make sure it's a fitting punishment." He smiled, pulling her in again for a slower, deeper kiss, the kind that filled her body with warmth.

"I love you." He headed in the opposite direction she needed to go.

She couldn't help but smile watching him leave. Who knew she would have met the one she wanted to spend the rest of her life with when they were so young? They had never really talked about their future, life after college, but she knew he thought about it almost as much as she did.

Staring out across the campus on the gray November morning, Alexis thought of her best friend, Nika, who was in Paris visiting her aunt and probably buying out all the stores. She laughed to herself, heading off to her next class, realizing she was more than just a little hungry having missed lunch. She would have to grab a small snack after her next class. As she picked up her pace, her mind wandered back to Aidan and his lecture, his voice playing in her head. He really was amazing to listen to. She couldn't understand why Sebastian had a problem with him. Sebastian wasn't the jealous type. Still, there *was* something about Aidan.

CHAPTER 2

Paris, France

Nika loved Paris and everything it had to offer, especially now. She needed to go out dancing tonight since her time in Paris was coming to an end. She had not spoken with her parents in weeks, unsure what to tell them exactly, so she decided not to worry about it tonight.

Standing in front of the mirror, she admired the new red dress she had purchased a few weeks ago, a short skirt that would flare while she moved on the dance floor. It was fitted through the body, displaying her perky breasts perfectly, and she decided to allow her fiery red locks to swirl about her shoulders freely. She added a glossy red color to her pouty lips to make them more inviting, then studied her reflection in the full-length mirror one last time. Her bright green eyes sparkled back at her, pleased with her appearance. She slipped on her three-inch black leather heels to complete her look, noting between the short skirt and high heels, her legs looked long, even though she was five-foot-nothing.

She grabbed her little black clutch and headed out the door, eager to get to the popular new club located just across town. She hailed a taxi, pleased at how quickly several showed up at the same time. She picked one, giving the driver the address. Initially she was amused by how often he admired her in the rearview mirror, but now she was annoyed. She *was* feeling a bit hungry, although she'd been told to behave herself. *He* had instructed her to become proficient with her new abilities but not draw too much attention in the process. She thought about the driver keeping his eyes on the road, and for the rest of the drive, he did.

Approaching the club, she looked out the window at the long line of people, desperate to get in, and as the taxi came to a stop, she smiled, knowing the line was nothing to concern herself with, at least not anymore. She had her ways. She paid the taxi driver, persuading him to open the door so she could exit the car. She really was starting to enjoy her new abilities. This mind control thing was so handy. She used to have to flirt like crazy, and now, just a mere thought was all it took to get what she wanted.

She walked towards the man standing on the desired side of the velvet rope. His eyes met hers, and he nodded silently, pulling the rope back so she could pass. A few complaints erupted behind her from the long line of patrons waiting desperately to get into the hottest nightclub in Paris. Walking through the doors, she was greeted by exquisite opulence everywhere she looked. Music filled the air, along with the distinctive aroma of different emotions, making the room intoxicating. The sweet and salty excitement of sex, along with the pungent odor of doubt and fear. The familiar smell of blood caught her attention, causing her eyes to shift immediately. Glancing towards the bar, she noticed the bartender quickly wrapping a towel around one of his hands. He had sliced it open cutting up garnish for the fancier drinks. Remembering her first kill, metallic melancholy filled her mind, and she licked her lips to regain her composure, closing her eyes for a second until she knew they were more normal. The club was dark, so she could certainly blame anything out of the ordinary on all the different lights flashing around the room, not to mention alcoholic beverages and possibly other assorted party favors. A few other random thoughts from some of the weaker-minded people in the room filled her head, and she focused on controlling their volumes. Reading and controlling minds were abilities she really couldn't wait to master because the first time she heard somebody's thoughts, she thought she was going crazy. Then *He* reassured her, the abilities to read and control minds were some of the more special gifts that not everyone of their kind had. It was impressed upon her how important it was to learn how to control them, how to turn them off and on, as well as how to magnify them to help keep herself safe. *Safe*. She felt invincible, although she knew that was not exactly true. Fire, beheading, and of course a stake through the heart. All were to be considered dangerous. Although beheading? Not really a concern today.

Nika found an available table that would allow her to see the entire room, as well as be seen. A waiter came over, and she ordered a glass of Bordeaux. She looked the waiter over for a moment . . . No, that would be too obvious. She needed to learn more patience, something she was always short on, even before the change. It was still in her nature to want things to come to her.

She had been born into a wealthy family, so getting what she wanted when she wanted it was what she was used to. *He* had told her she should also hone her hunting skills, but she really didn't see the point, or the need. It just sounded like a lot of work, and that just wasn't who she was. She still believed they would come to her, now more than ever.

The waiter returned quickly with her wine, and she sat back, enjoying all the sights and sounds in the club. Several of the men in the room wanted her, curiosity driving them crazy over why such a beautiful woman was sitting alone. One smiled at her, and she smiled back, quickly looking away and taking another sip of wine. After all, she didn't want to appear too eager. Setting her glass down, she smiled to herself, feeling his presence beside her, his desire filling her head. She paused a moment before looking up at him.

"Good evening. My name is Lamar."

She smiled. "Hello."

"I was wondering if I might join you this evening."

"Yes, that would be lovely."

The man sat across from her, smiling as he studied her. Nika could tell from the way the man was dressed he either came from money or made a good living. The lines of his clothes were tailored to fit his body, neatly pressed as well.

"What is your name?" he asked, his French accent thick with eagerness.

"Nika."

"You are American, yes?"

"Yes, I am."

"What brings such a beautiful American to Paris?"

"I'm here visiting my aunt and sightseeing." She already knew what he wanted. She took another sip of her wine, carefully licking her lips. The wine was good, but her hunger was growing.

"Would you like to dance?" he asked.

"That would be nice."

The smell of his desire increased as he escorted her to the dance floor. They danced to a few fast songs, and when a slow song started, he grabbed her, pulling her close to his body. She complied, enjoying the attention and his warmth, assessing how the rest of the evening would go. He was not very tall, and that would be useful later. He looked deep into her eyes before stealing a kiss. It was time. Her hunger was starting to get the better of her, and she didn't want to lose control.

Making their way back to the table, Lamar's excitement trickled across the air, tickling her tongue with the promise of salty sweetness.

"I must go now," she declared, smiling up at him, knowing he was not ready to say good-bye. "I've enjoyed myself, but I have a full schedule tomorrow."

"My flat is just around the corner." Hesitation in his voice. He wasn't ready to say good night. "Would you be interested in a nightcap?"

She paused a moment, as if she were really contemplating his invitation, allowing his excitement to build. "I suppose that couldn't hurt since you're just around the corner."

They left the club, strolling down the sidewalk and making small talk along the way. The night air was crisp and full of promise. His pace slowed before he stopped in front of a building.

"Here we are," he announced, offering his hand.

She smiled, taking it as she followed him up to the door. He entered a code on the box affixed to the wall. A buzzing noise and a click indicated the door had unlocked. He led her up the stairs to the third floor, watching her expression. Opening the door, he stepped back, allowing her to enter his flat first. Nika studied the dimly lit space simply furnished with a large sofa and a round coffee table with an assortment of magazines spread out across the top. A tall standing floor lamp in the far corner of the living room offered the only light source, making the basic beige walls seem even more boring, despite the fact that there were a few art pieces on them. None of the pieces had much color in them, which was typical for a single young man. There was a cozy kitchenette with one wall of cabinets and a smaller than standard range for cooking. A small table with a couple of chairs around it, where he ate his meals, filled the rest of the space. A hint of sandalwood musk lingered in the air from the candles recently lit, perhaps earlier that evening or for another guest last night.

The flat was dim and dreary, much like she figured Lamar was, so she would make this quick to avoid becoming bored.

The front door closed behind her. When she turned to face him, he picked her up and spun her, pressing her body firmly against the back of the door. His mouth suddenly devoured hers, and she didn't fight him. She wanted him excited. It made the task at hand more enjoyable. The kiss was deep, his taste intoxicating, and if she needed to breathe, it might have been an issue. Thankfully, it was not.

He pulled back from her, breathing heavy, his eyes dilated from excitement. "I knew you would be fun."

She smiled coyly. "You have no idea."

"Why don't you make yourself comfortable? I'll be right back."

"Sounds wonderful," she replied.

He headed off into the bedroom, and when she heard a door close in the distance, she reached behind her, locking the front door. She hated interruptions. Slipping her shoes off, she walked across the flat into the bedroom, disrobing along the way.

Moments later, he opened the bathroom door and walked across the room, when he noticed her clothing on the floor. He stopped dead in his tracks and spun around to face the bed. There she was, standing on top of the bed, leaning against the wall, naked, a mischievous smile playing across her stained pouty lips. His breath caught in his throat and his eyes widened. She was flawless. Perfect pale skin from head to toe, except for the pink nipples pushing firmly against the air and the patch of fire below, a perfect match to the fiery locks on her head.

With his eyes locked on her, he struggled to remove his clothing as fast as possible without ripping them. He stepped up on the bed, walking slowly towards her, afraid she might change her mind if he approached too quickly.

The closer he got, the more she could feel her excitement taking over. He was warm and ready, but she was only interested in his warmth.

"My god, you are beautiful," he said, staring deep into her eyes.

"Thank you, for everything." She smiled, revealing her lengthy fangs. She loved this part.

Frozen in place, his face ashen with fear, she grabbed him by the shoulders to spin him around before pushing him back against the wall. The strength of her hands held him in place as she leapt forward, sinking her teeth into the right side of his neck, her hunger demanding every drop. His breathing slowed, and the once pounding sound of his heartbeat softened in her head, as did his thoughts, until there was nothing but silence.

Sated, she pulled back from the lifeless body, holding it at arm's length, studying the face for a moment. The jaw had dropped open, and the eyes were completely shut now. She wondered if next time she should give herself the opportunity to enjoy everything a man had to offer. Her eyes traveled down the length of the body to the frozen readiness, and she smiled. Definitely.

Releasing her grip, she stepped back, watching the body slide down the wall into a seated position, the head falling to one side. She needed a shower. She turned and walked to the edge of the bed, feeling revived as she stepped down to the floor.

Her lips, caked with blood, curled into a wicked and satisfied smile. Casually strolling towards the bathroom, she discovered blood spatter across her breasts and, using her fingers to collect what she had missed, she licked them clean as she walked through the door to the bathroom. She flipped the light on with her elbow, amazed blood could dry so quickly. She turned the water on in the shower and waited for it to warm up enough before stepping in. The waterfall-style showerhead generously spilled water over her body, turning the caked-on blood back into a slick, sticky mess cascading down her body. She reached for the bar of soap on the ledge, generously lathering herself up from head to toe before rinsing until the water ran clean. She closed her eyes, a wave of warmth filling her normally cold body. The hot water and the memory of the immortal gift she had been given prolonged her bliss.

She'd been scared at first when *He* approached her, informing her of his plan, explaining to her just how important she was to him. *He* explained everything, empathizing with how she had felt for years, the personal frustrations she had never told anyone, except her best friend. Nika knew she had made the right decision. Besides, what idiot would pass up the opportunity to stay young and beautiful forever?

She finished her shower, stepping out to dry herself off with a fresh towel she found in the armoire. She looked in the cabinet under the sink and found a hair dryer. When her hair was dry, she put everything away and walked back into the bedroom. She dressed quickly, realizing she would be heading back to Seattle in about a week and she still had a million things to do.

Nika walked towards the living room, casting one last glance over her shoulder to survey the fun she had. The room had been turned from boring beige tones into wonderful random patterns of deep garnet and bright red. She smiled to herself, reaching for the doorknob.

"I've always enjoyed adding a splash of color wherever I go," she said out loud, laughing as she entered the hallway.

CHAPTER 3

Seattle

Memories flooded her mind as Alexis walked through the front door of the house where she lived with her grandmother. The smell of warm cooking sherry never failed to make her smile. Plus, she could smell that Gram had made her favorite dinner, chicken Kiev with brown rice. Alexis could also smell apple cobbler warming in the oven. Setting her book bag down next to a small table in the entryway across from the door, she slipped her coat off, hanging it on the coatrack. Walking through the living room and rounding the corner to the dining room, she saw her grandmother had set the table with her best crystal and china. The table was draped in a beautiful antique white lace tablecloth, with black cloth napkins trimmed in matching lace. In the center of the table were the roses Sebastian had given her that morning when he picked her up for school, and lit candles flanked the bouquet. The wine had been poured and the salads set to the left of the dinner plates.

Charlotte McCree was all about tradition, teaching her granddaughter everything her mother had passed down to her many years ago. She'd taught Alexis how to set a formal table, and it always made her smile to see the joy in her granddaughter's eyes, knowing she was happy to carry on those traditions.

Gram was standing in the doorway of the dining room, holding a plate in each hand with steam rising rapidly over the food, her blue eyes sparkling as always, and her salt-and-pepper hair neatly combed in place.

"Everything looks so beautiful and smells delicious. Thank you for making my favorite," Alexis said.

"You are welcome, my dear girl. Let's sit down and eat before it gets cold. How was your day?" Gram asked, setting a plate in front of Alexis, who was already in her chair. Missing lunch was a bad idea. She was starving.

"There was a lecture today at school for Art History with a guest speaker, Mr. Aidan Drake, and he was incredible, so well-spoken and articulate. He's extremely knowledgeable on all periods and has traveled the world building his own personal collection that I would love to see." She paused for a moment, placing her napkin in her lap. "It was weird though. I got the feeling Sebastian didn't really like him."

"What makes you say that?"

"He just seemed a bit cold and standoffish, unfriendly even when I introduced him to Aidan. It was odd, even after Aidan invited us to attend the reopening of the gallery just a few blocks from here this Saturday, Sebastian still didn't warm up to him."

"That *is* odd," Gram replied.

"I agree," she said before pausing to look at the food in front of her. "This looks so good, like always."

"I'm glad you like it. You act like you haven't eaten in a week." She studied her granddaughter as she attacked her plate.

"Well," Alexis began, "I kind of missed lunch today because I lost track of time with Mr. Drake after the lecture."

Her grandmother simply smiled, shaking her head. "Well, eat up because I also made your favorite dessert. Plus, there should be enough leftovers for the next couple of days. Tomorrow I'm driving down to Oregon to meet up with a few old friends. I should be back Sunday night."

"Oregon? Is everything okay?"

"Oh yes, everything is fine. We just haven't seen each other in some time, and it's sort of middle ground, so to speak. Just going to do some catching up," Gram stated with a smile.

"I've never stayed alone in the house before, but don't worry. I promise, no wild parties."

"I'm sure you'll be fine, dear. I figured you would probably just have Sebastian over." Gram winked.

Alexis stopped eating for a moment, glancing at her grandmother, who was smiling. She dropped her eyes, blush filling her cheeks.

"It's okay, dear. I remember what it was like to be a young girl in love," she said.

After dinner, Alexis helped Gram clean off the table, putting the dirty dishes in the dishwasher. There really wasn't too much work to do to clean up because Gram cleaned as she cooked. Alexis pulled the apple cobbler from the oven, setting it on the stove top as her grandmother poured a cup of coffee for each of them. Together they carried the coffee and cobbler back into the dining room. They sat and continued chatting about the day's events, Alexis telling Gram more about the lecture and the different slides that were shown, the ones she could remember. Another hour passed before they both realized it was getting late.

"I'll be leaving around six a.m., so we probably won't see each other in the morning," Gram announced as she stood to carry the rest of the dirty dishes into the kitchen.

"Thank you for the delicious dinner," Alexis said, following her grandmother into the kitchen. She watched as Gram added the dishes to the dishwasher and started it.

"I have something for you. Come with me," Gram said, walking through the living room and upstairs. Alexis followed her down the hallway to Gram's room, pausing for a moment just outside the doorway.

"What is it?" she asked before entering, watching as her grandmother walked over to her dresser and opened her jewelry box. Alexis took a few more steps, stopping next to the large chest that sat at the foot of the bed. She glanced down at the top of the chest, and she could tell it was incredibly old, probably a family heirloom. Staring at it, she realized she had always wondered what was in that big old chest. It was always locked, and she remembered asking her grandmother many years ago when she first moved in, what was in the chest. "Different things" was the only answer ever given.

Gram turned around holding up an oval-shaped gold locket hanging from an eighteen-inch chain. The locket was about one inch by one and a half inches in size, and in the center, it had a pear-shaped imperial topaz surrounded by eight sparkling rose-cut diamonds that formed a teardrop halo. There were additional smaller diamonds resting in between the larger ones, providing extra sparkle to all the stones.

"Oh, Gram, it's beautiful!" Walking slowly over, Alexis reached out her right hand, and Gram placed the locket in her open palm. Gram opened the front of the locket, revealing a picture of Alexis's parents inside. Her eyes welled up, and Alexis couldn't stop the tears from rolling down her cheeks. Gram leaned over, gently brushing the tears away, dropping a kiss on her granddaughter's cheek.

"Your parents would be *so* proud of you."

Alexis looked up at Gram.

"I know *I* am."

"I miss them so much," Alexis declared.

Alexis was six years old when she lost her parents in a car accident. They were living in California at the time and getting ready to move to Washington State, where her grandmother lived. Her parents had found a house and would have been driving up a few days later to join her. Alexis loved visiting Gram in Seattle during the summers. It wasn't as hot as California, although she did miss Sebastian and his family when she was visiting Gram.

A day after they arrived in Seattle, Gram got a call with the awful news: her daughter, Joanna, and her son-in-law, Nathaniel, had been killed. Alexis was devastated and scared, but together, she and her grandmother formed a closer bond.

Gram raised her, supporting everything Alexis was passionate about, like dancing and art. Gram was happy to help when it came to sewing costumes for all her dance recitals, cheering her on from the front row.

A few years later, Sebastian and his family moved to Washington State, getting a house two miles away from Gram's. Alexis and Sebastian had not seen each other in a few years, but their connection to one another was undeniable. Sebastian was eleven years old and really into martial arts. He still made time to see Alexis on a regular basis, and she was thrilled he was back in her life.

After high school, Gram encouraged Alexis to continue her education, studying art history at the university, and also nurturing the relationship she had developed with Sebastian, knowing the two belonged together.

Alexis gave her grandmother a hug, turning so she could put the locket on her. As soon as it contacted her skin it felt warm and familiar like it was a part of her. Gram steered her over to the mirror above the dresser so Alexis could admire the locket.

"It's so beautiful, and it looks very old."

"Well," Gram chuckled, "you could say that. It once belonged to your great-grandmother, my mother. She was a strong, beautiful woman just like you, who was also born in November."

"I am *so* honored by this; I will treasure it always."

"I know you will, dear," Gram said, hugging her granddaughter again. "Now, off to bed you go, or at least to your room. I've got an early day and I need to get some sleep."

"Good night," Alexis said, heading out the door.

"Good night, sweet girl," Gram said. "I love you."

"I love you too," she said as Gram closed her door.

She headed down the hall to her own room, shutting the door behind her. She walked over to her bed and sat down, turning the radio on at the same time. She was greeted by "Bette Davis Eyes" by Kim Carnes. The song had a synthesizer-based arrangement Alexis really liked, and she loved Carnes's rough, raspy vocal style. She was different from anybody else, just like Bette herself. Alexis lay back on her bed, closing her eyes while the music filled her mind. She smiled, reaching up with her right hand to hold the locket between her thumb and forefinger. She lay there until the song ended and a commercial came on. She got off her bed, walking over to her dresser, and carefully removed the locket from her neck and placed it inside her jewelry box. She admired it, slowly lowering the lid of the box when the center of the topaz seemed to put out a little more shine for a moment. Then the flare of light was gone. Lifting the lid all the way up, she shook her head, staring at the topaz a moment before closing the top. She felt a bit lightheaded. It had been a long day and she was tired.

After she changed, she went into the bathroom to wash her face and brush her teeth. She studied her reflection in the mirror for a moment. Twenty-one years old. *Where did the time go?* She laughed, turning away from the mirror to head back to her room.

She closed the door and climbed into bed, reaching over to her nightstand to turn off the radio and the light. *Tomorrow is another day, full of possibilities,* she thought as she closed her eyes and drifted off to sleep.

CHAPTER 4

Self-defense was no joke, especially working out with Sebastian and his best friend, Josh. Alexis only had two classes on Thursdays, so she would run home and change clothes, grabbing a quick bite to eat before heading over to the gym Josh owned. She had been training with them for the last six months, learning how to defend herself, and discovered it really could be an intense workout.

Arriving at the gym around two p.m., she walked through the door, noticing the guys were already working hard, making it look so easy. Learning martial arts was not difficult for Alexis since she had studied dance for years. Learning the body mechanics and remembering the combinations was easy. The challenge was remembering to roll her hip over instead of keeping it down and not to point her toe on every type of kick. She had also learned it was completely different kicking air as opposed to kicking a bag. Big difference! The air didn't knock you on your ass when you did it wrong. She smiled to herself remembering the bag coming back a few times to knock her off her feet. All part of the learning curve.

The gym was large, with a variety of things to do from free weights and a couple of stationary bikes to heavy bags and speed bags. There was also a ring located in the center of the gym for sparring. A few long, narrow windows along the top of the far wall could be cracked to let fresh air in or the musty smell of sweat out. The smell didn't really bother Alexis anymore. She was used to it by now.

Sebastian ran over when he saw her, dropping a kiss on her left cheek. "Hey there, fresh-faced girl." His face was a little flushed, covered in perspiration, and she could tell he was completely warmed up.

"Hey there, yourself," she said back with a big smile.

"Looks like you're ready to work out," Josh said, wandering over. He looked like he was ready for round two.

Josh was a few inches taller than Sebastian, but it wasn't just that he was six foot four. He had long arms and legs, which made his reach, combined with his speed, deadly. His dark brown hair was cut shorter on the sides and normally spiked across the top. His blue-gray eyes seemed distant most of the time, making you wonder what was going on in his head or perhaps what he might have seen in his short lifetime. Alexis had never heard of Josh dating anybody. He was extremely attractive, looking like a model most of the time, yet he could be terribly aloof, which might make him seem mysterious to one girl or unfriendly to another.

Sebastian and Josh had met in the military. They were more like brothers than friends, bonding over the fact that they had both grown up taking martial arts, competing throughout their adolescent years, earning them nicknames; Sebastian was known as "The Scotsman" and Josh was known as "Reaper," indicating just how skilled he was. Their skills were well above average, making both great instructors. "So, what are you up for today?" Sebastian asked.

"I wanted to get stretched out and warmed up, then work the heavy bag a bit, maybe a little sparring," she replied.

"Stretched out?" Josh teased. "*Please*, Alexis. All those years of dance have made you extremely flexible."

Alexis laughed. "You're one to talk, Mr. Reaper," she retorted, hands on her hips.

Josh smiled, standing a bit taller than before. "Not Mister. Just Reaper," he said matter-of-factly.

"All right, you two," Sebastian said playfully, stepping between them like a referee. "Don't make me separate you before you even get in the ring."

"What?" Alexis exclaimed, looking nervously at Sebastian, then Josh. "I'm going to be sparring with Josh today?"

"Well, yeah," Sebastian replied. "I gotta leave here in about fifteen minutes to help my dad. Besides, I want Josh to work with you on your ground game. He's been working with me, and he's more proficient than I am at breaking down the moves."

Alexis continued looking nervously at Josh. "Okay."

"Don't worry, Alexis," Josh said, a wicked smile on his handsome face. "I promise to be gentle."

"Hey, man." Sebastian laughed. "Don't scare her, and play nice."

"She'll be fine," Josh stated.

Alexis wasn't so sure. She had spent enough time around Josh, but Sebastian was always there, like a buffer. She had only known Josh for about two years, and there had been times she caught him studying her, not in a way that scared her, more like he was trying to figure her out. Most of the time he was a man of few words, but there was an intensity behind his silence that could be unnerving if you didn't know him. Thankfully, she did know him or at least was reassured knowing Sebastian knew him. Sebastian trusted him, and that was good enough for her.

Sebastian smiled and winked at her. He stepped forward and whispered in her ear, "You'll be fine." He dropped another kiss on her cheek before running off to the locker room to shower.

"Okay, girlie," Josh said, smiling. "Let's get you warmed up."

Alexis stared at him for a moment before walking over to the mats in the corner of the gym, setting her bag down out of the way. She started with some jumping jacks and some high knees, running in place to get her blood flowing before dropping down to the mats to get stretched out. After about fifteen minutes, she looked up to see Sebastian waving good-bye as he headed out the door. She stood up, reaching her arms across her body to stretch her shoulders, one at a time. She wasn't sure why she was so nervous. They were the only two people left in the gym now, and she knew Josh would never hurt her, but his skill level was a bit unnerving when she thought about it. She had seen him spar with Sebastian before, and although at first they seemed evenly matched, in the end, Josh made Sebastian submit using an arm bar.

Josh was already inside the ring. Alexis stepped in to join him. "What exactly are we going to be working on today?" she asked.

"Sebastian and I were talking about how many young women have been disappearing lately, so we thought arming you with a higher level of defensive training would be good," he replied. Josh was referring to several prostitutes who had disappeared in the Seattle area recently.

"You really think it's necessary?" she asked. "I mean, I'm not a sex worker, so I should be safe."

"That's true, but it's still a good idea," he replied. "I believe everybody should know how to handle themselves. I really want to focus on your abilities, hone your strengths."

"And what strengths are those?"

"Your flexibility for one. You haven't taken dance in years, yet you have managed to maintain your flexibility. We can use that to your advantage. Your legs are also incredibly strong, which is a huge advantage, especially when it comes to the ground game. It's all in the hips."

"Okay," she replied. "How should we start?"

"Let's start with you throwing some kicks." Josh walked to the opposite end of the ring, where he picked up a couple of focus paddles and walked back. "We'll start with alternating roundhouse kicks, traveling diagonally across the ring from this corner to that one," he said, gesturing back to the opposite side of the ring.

He took a few steps back, extending his arm and holding the paddle out about waist high for her. Alexis got into a fighting stance ready to execute the first kick. She pivoted on her right foot, striking the paddle with her left foot, and then she planted her left foot to pivot around to strike the other paddle with her right foot on the next kick. They traveled from one side of the ring to the other, Alexis throwing one kick after another. It got the heart rate up. Once they reached the opposite corner, they traded places. This time Josh held the paddle up a little higher, face level for her.

Again, they traveled across the ring, Alexis throwing alternating roundhouse kicks, striking the paddle every time. Afterward, they worked on a variety of punching combinations. She loved her right cross, although she was also fond of her jab, and it didn't matter which side. She felt strong and confident in her abilities, thanks to the guys. They had trained her well.

Josh tossed the smaller paddle off to the side and picked up a larger pad. He got into position so she could work on her sidekicks. He studied her for a moment, admiring how much power and beauty she had. It was getting more difficult to keep his emotions in check when he was around her, and being alone with her certainly didn't help, but Sebastian was his best friend, and he would never do anything to disrespect their relationship.

In the military, he and Sebastian had both decided to do active duty for two years and then be in the Reserves. They were also selected for a special unit because of their backgrounds. They developed a friendship quickly, becoming more like brothers than friends.

After two years, Sebastian decided he wanted to go to college, while Josh decided to work at a nightclub as a bouncer, making money until he figured out exactly what he wanted to do. He had been able to buy the gym and live there, keeping his living expenses down. He didn't date much, a girl here and there but they didn't seem to hold his interest. They just didn't compare to *her*. He couldn't help but wonder what just one kiss would be like. A sudden impact sent him flying back into the ropes behind him.

"Oh my god!" Alexis exclaimed. "Are you okay?"

He shook it off, trying to regain his composure. Josh just looked at her, stepping out of the ropes with the pad. "I'm good, and so was that kick." They both laughed.

Alexis was proud of herself, grinning from ear to ear. "You sure you're okay, Sparky?" she asked, stifling a laugh.

"I am," he said, attempting to hide a smile. "I'd say it's time to move on to your ground game." Josh tossed the large pad away from him and walked to the center of the ring.

Alexis paused for a moment. "I'm so sweaty right now," she said. "Are you sure?"

Josh shook his head, grinning at her. "Come on, little one. Wipe your brow and let's go."

"*Little one*," she repeated with a smirk.

"That was for the Sparky remark," he said, smiling. "Let's go."

"Hang on," she said, turning her back for a moment. She pulled off her sweatshirt, wiping her face with it before tossing it in the corner of the ring. Thankfully, she had on a black tank top underneath, over her sports bra. She walked over to join him, sitting on the floor in the middle of the ring. She sat down, facing him with her legs crossed. His face was flushed, his blue-gray eyes watching her. They stared at each other for a moment. "Please don't hurt me," she said softly.

Josh couldn't help laughing out loud. "I have no intentions of hurting you, but I want to make sure nobody else can either. Okay?"

"Okay," she said, laughing nervously.

For the next hour, Josh taught her the basics of how to escape different ground positions if she was in the bottom position. They worked on everything from what to do if somebody knocks you down to how to defend and escape if somebody were on top of you. Alexis was amazed by how much knowledge Josh had and how easy it was to follow what he was showing her. They ran through the different scenarios several times, and he would speed up the attack for a faster response from her, making sure the muscle memory was being developed. Some of the positions involved being face-to-face with each other, making her feel a bit self-conscious because of how sweaty she was. Fortunately, she had no idea how hard Josh's heart was beating being so close to her. When training was over, they were both a sweaty mess, yet she was still the most beautiful girl he had ever seen.

They both stepped down out of the ring and walked over to the mats. Alexis sat down and started stretching what she knew were going to be sore muscles. She sighed and Josh laughed.

"Tired?"

"Yes, and I can't wait to get home and soak in a hot bath," she said.

"You did well today," he said. "How do you feel about what you learned?"

"Pretty good," she answered. "I guess I didn't realize exactly what you meant when you said 'ground game.'"

"We both wanted you to be prepared for anything," he said. "Next time we'll make it a little more aggressive, takedowns and more on escapes. How does that sound?"

"Scary, but I'm willing. I guess I would much rather have the edge in that type of situation than rely on luck."

"That's a good way to think of it," he said. "Being prepared for the worst is always the best."

Alexis stared at him, trying not to laugh.

"Damn, that really sounded like a fortune cookie, didn't it?" he asked.

Alexis laughed. "It did, but I understand what you meant. Thanks again, Josh. I should get going," she said, standing. She retrieved her sweatshirt from inside the ring, pulling it on over her head. She pulled her coat on, and when she turned around again, Josh was on his feet. Together they walked towards the door.

"I'm surprised there weren't more people here," she said.

"There will be later tonight," he declared. "Some of my regulars come in around six p.m. and work out hard before going to bed. I guess it helps them sleep."

"I know that won't be a problem for me tonight," she said.

"Do you want me to walk you to your car?" he asked.

"No," she replied. "I'm just right there," she said, pointing to the right of the door. "Night."

"Good night," he said. He watched as she walked out the door and to her car. Damn his luck that Sebastian found her first.

CHAPTER 5

There was almost nothing in the world that couldn't be resolved by the power of a hot bath. It had been a long day, and all Alexis could think about was relaxing in the tub. Having the house to herself was just a bonus. She wandered into the bathroom, turning the light on before walking over to the bathtub. She turned the water on and adjusted the temperature as the tub began to fill.

Alexis exhaled as she began peeling her workout clothes off her body, tossing them into the dirty-clothes hamper. Glancing at the tub, she was happy to see it was almost to her liking. She opened a drawer at the end of the vanity and pulled out a box of matches. She lit several candles, varying in size, displayed throughout the bathroom. Gram had great taste in accessories, and she and Alexis had gone shopping together to find the different candle holders for the bathroom and the rest of the house.

It was a good-size bathroom, and it was always amazing to Alexis just how much heat all the candles created. There were a few tall ones near the window, as well as a collection across the back of the vanity countertop and a large candle displayed on the back of the toilet.

After all the candles were lit, she reached down to open the door on the front of the vanity. She pulled a cassette player out, setting it on the countertop. She pressed *Rewind* and waited until she heard the familiar click indicating the tape was at the beginning. She pushed *Play*, adjusting the volume to make sure it wouldn't be too loud, remembering how the song would build.

She turned the water off and the overhead light, admiring the glow from the warmth of candlelight, readjusting her hair on top of her head as she sighed. Placing her left hand on the front wall over the tub, she wiped her feet off a few times on the bathmat before carefully stepping into the water. The temperature was nice and hot, sending goosebumps up her legs, just above her ankles. She closed her eyes, letting her head fall back, her feet and ankles getting used to the hot temperature of the water. She took a step back and leaned forward to reach for the edge of the tub, easing herself down into the water, then inching forward a bit before she reclined back to rest against the slope of the tub, and she sighed again.

Alexis closed her eyes, exhaling a long slow breath as Ravel's "Boléro" softly filled the air. Her breathing calmed, her mind wandering to the last time she had heard the song play. A soft moan escaped her lips, "Mm, Sebastian," as she rubbed her feet together under the water, memories of dance class from years ago coming back to her. She would come home and soak her feet after pointe class, loving and hating it at the same time. Deep in thought, she was starting to drift off when a noise made her jump. She looked over to see Sebastian entering the bathroom.

"I'm sorry, babe, I didn't mean to startle you," he said. "I let myself in. I hope you don't mind."

"Not at all," she said, leaning over as he knelt to greet her lips with his. He smelled so good.

"I didn't mean to interrupt your bath. Should I wait outside?"

"Or . . ." she said, a wicked smile on her face, "you could join me."

Sebastian stood, taking a step back. He smiled down at her. "Well, how can I say no to that?"

She studied him as he undressed, his body well developed from martial arts, perfectly balanced in form from head to toe, with strength and power. He carefully stepped into the tub behind her, and she slid forward to make room for him. He reached for the outside edge of the tub for balance, carefully sliding in behind her. The water level rose quickly, almost spilling out over the edge of the tub. Once nestled down in the tub, he stretched his legs out on either side of her hips. He gently reached around and placed his right hand on her stomach, pulling her backward, right up against the front of him, and Alexis giggled a bit as the water sloshed around. She leaned back, settling comfortably into his firm chest, their bodies molding together like pieces of a puzzle.

Alexis allowed her head to fall back against his shoulder and smiled as Sebastian kissed her just behind her right ear. Any remaining stress from the day slipped away, and all she felt now was safe and warm. She moved her left hand from the outside edge of the tub, placing it over his hand on her stomach, their fingers intertwining. She thought about how perfect everything was in her life.

"What are you thinking about?" he asked quietly.

"How happy I am," she replied. "You make me happy."

He kissed her neck and cheek as he pulled her tighter to his body. "You make me happy, Alexis."

They sat quietly in each other's embrace as the music played on, eventually stirring their deepest desires. He kissed the back of her neck again, his hands encircling her breasts, gently caressing them, and she moaned, stretching her neck back to catch his right earlobe between her lips.

"Sebastian?" she whispered. "I don't think we have enough room here for what you have in mind."

"Then it sounds like bath time is over," he replied. He gently slid her forward enough so he could stand and step out of the tub. She reached forward, flipping the trip lever on the tub so it would drain. She looked up to find a hand out to help her stand.

She carefully stepped out of the tub, and Sebastian pulled her in for a deep kiss. She stretched her arms up around his neck, feeling his strong hands sliding down over the curves of her hips, then grasping her legs to pick her up and carry her over to the countertop. The cold countertop was a drastic contrast to the hot tub she had just been in, but soon her entire body was filled with heat as the sounds of the tub draining and the music building fell away in the background until it was just them.

CHAPTER 6

Charlotte McCree got out of her car and walked across the parking lot towards the diner. It was late Friday afternoon, and she had an hour before her next meeting, a meeting she knew she was going to need coffee to get through. It wasn't like these people were unreasonable, they were just—no, wait, they really were unreasonable. Always wanting things to go and be done their way. They gave no thought to whom their decisions would affect or what the consequences of those decisions might be. Charlotte had worked hard to raise her granddaughter right, allowing her to blossom into the bright young woman she had become, while protecting her from all harm that could come her way. Now these people wanted to get involved, possibly exposing her to the most dangerous . . .

Charlotte stopped just outside the door of the diner. She listened carefully, looking towards the side of the building, the alley between the diner and the business beside it.

"*Charlotte?*" a soft voice called to her.

She looked around but didn't see anybody. Mindlessly, she felt herself being drawn away from entering the diner. She moved in the direction of the voice. The side of the building cast a shadow at the entrance to the alley, causing a chill to run through her body. She reached up and pulled the collar of her winter coat tighter to the front of her neck. Moving further down the alley, she saw a figure hunched over slightly, the face half covered by the side of the jacket it was wearing.

"Are you all right?" Charlotte asked.

A throaty laugh came from the figure, and Charlotte stopped suddenly, realizing she had made a huge mistake. She began taking steps backward, slowly creating distance between her and the figure, when it disappeared right before her eyes. She turned to exit the shadows, but a force came out of nowhere, pushing her body against the side of the building, causing her to drop her car keys and forcing the rest of the air out of her lunges. When she opened her eyes again, the cloaked face was now inches from her own.

"You thought you were being *so* clever, didn't you, Charlotte?"

She stared back into the face, the sharp features peering out from the hood. "You're too late," she said, her voice trembling. "She is safe now."

"*She* will never be safe again," the voice whispered.

It was the last thing Charlotte heard.

CHAPTER 7

Saturday morning arrived and Alexis could hardly contain her excitement, waking up around eight a.m., grateful she had been able to sleep in a bit. She bounded out of bed, slipping into some sweats and a T-shirt before heading downstairs to the kitchen, pausing at the stereo first. She needed music, something to dance to. She pushed the power button on the stereo and switched the dial to find her favorite station. Music was like a drug for Alexis, and thankfully, the only one. Her passion for music started at a young age, probably due to her being a dancer. She always had to have music on.

The tuner found her station, playing "Hot in the City" by Billy Idol just as the wind died and the girls start singing. It was a slower song, so not really what she was looking for, but she let it play while she moved towards the kitchen, hoping a faster song would come on soon. She started a pot of coffee and decided to make an omelet for breakfast. Opening the refrigerator, she pulled out the eggs, milk, and leftover chicken Kiev, which would make for an interesting omelet. From the other room, she heard the music change. "Heart of Glass" by Blondie started playing, which really helped, beating the eggs and milk to the beat. Once everything was in the skillet, she added bread to the toaster and retrieved the creamer from the refrigerator to add to her coffee. Her mind wandered to that evening's upcoming events. Dinner and the gallery opening. Smiling, she folded her breakfast mix into a beautiful omelet, carefully dishing it out onto a plate. She grabbed her toast when it popped up and added some butter to it and coffee to her cup.

She carried everything to the breakfast room table, setting it down, when she heard a knock at the front door. Walking through the living room, she turned the music down slightly, noticing the time on the grandfather clock sitting in the corner of the room. It was 8:45 a.m., a little early for company. Walking over to the front door, she peered through the peephole to see a UPS cap. She opened the door slowly.

"Alexis McBain?" he asked.

"That's me," she answered.

"Sign here, please," he said, handing her the tablet and pen.

Alexis signed on the line and handed them back to the man. He handed her a UPS envelope.

"Thank you."

"Have a nice day," he said with a smile before heading back to his truck.

She closed the door and locked it before walking back to her breakfast. She sat down and opened the envelope, finding a note from Sebastian.

Alexis,

A day of beauty, for my beauty. Your appointment at "The Spa" starts at 10:00 a.m. I will pick you up from your house at 6:00 p.m.

Love always,

Sebastian

Alexis smiled, setting the note and envelope aside to focus on her breakfast. It was fast approaching nine a.m., and she still needed to eat and shower.

After she finished her breakfast, she put the dishes in the dishwasher and wiped the countertops down. She ran upstairs to shower and dress, throwing on a pair of jeans, a T-shirt, and sneakers before pulling her hair back in a ponytail. Slipping on her black leather jacket and black boots, she grabbed her wallet and keys, as well as the note with the address to the spa from the table by the front door. Once in the car, she pulled out a map and figured out the best route.

After her wonderful spa day, Alexis stopped at a little deli on the way home to grab a small bite to eat. She had not eaten anything since breakfast, but she didn't want to spoil her appetite for dinner. She had no idea where Sebastian was taking her, but she knew it would be nice. She headed home to get ready for the evening. She felt sufficiently pampered after a massage, facial, manicure, and pedicure.

Putting her makeup on, she added a little more color to her eyes since it was a special occasion. She loved working with neutral tones, adding a touch of a copper on the outside corner of her upper lids. Her lipstick was called "Raisin," one of her favorite shades, but she had never seen a raisin that color. Satisfied with her makeup, she ran a brush briskly through her long layers, sweeping her hair up and pinning it on her head, leaving a few wispy strands here and there. She walked back into her room to get dressed, stepping into her closet to retrieve the black lace cocktail dress her best friend, Nika, had sent her from Paris. Nika had the best taste in clothes and always knew what looked good on Alexis, or anybody else for that matter. Alexis often thought her best friend could be a personal shopper, but Nika had other ideas for her talents and abilities. Alexis had always wanted to go to Paris, mostly for the art and architecture, not so much for the shopping. Then again, Paris was known for being the fashion capital of the world.

She carefully pulled the dress over her head, making sure not to disturb her hair and makeup. Slipping her heels on, she walked over to her jewelry box to add her topaz studs and the locket to complete her look for the evening. Alexis stepped over to look at herself in the full-length mirror hanging on the back of the closet door, admiring her new dress. It followed the lines of her body perfectly without being too tight. The black lace was exquisite over a neutral background, and the sweetheart neckline was perfect with the locket. *Not bad*, she thought. All those years of dance had really paid off. She had been blessed with an athletic build for the most part, and when puberty hit, nature added curves in all the right places. Her eyes traveled the full length of the image staring back at her, when again she thought she saw the center of the topaz shine brighter than before. She shook her head, reaching up to touch the locket. Perhaps it was her parents saying hello. Alexis laughed out loud. Did she really believe in that kind of stuff? Closing the closet door, she walked over to her bed to retrieve her chocolate-brown wrap and matching purse before heading downstairs to the living room.

CHAPTER 8

It was 5:59 p.m. when Alexis heard a knock on the door. She opened it to find Sebastian standing before her in a tailored black suit, causing her heartbeat to quicken. The silk tie and matching handkerchief had a baroque pattern in the background with diagonal golden-brown stripes, and the color of the stripes was a perfect match to the imperial topaz in the locket. They both smiled, greeting each other with a kiss. Sebastian slipped his hands around her waist, his fingertips caressing her back. Even with two-and-a-half-inch heels on, she still had to look up into his eyes, but she didn't mind. She loved how tall he was. It made her feel safe.

"You look beautiful," he said, stepping back to admire her.

"Thank you," she replied. "You look great, and I can't believe how well your tie matches my locket."

"I asked your grandmother what color tie I should wear, and she showed me the locket," he responded sheepishly.

"Sneaky."

"That's how they trained me," he announced proudly. "You ready?"

"Yes, just let me grab my wrap and purse," she replied.

Sebastian helped Alexis with her wrap, dropping a kiss on the back of her neck before draping the wrap across her shoulders. She shivered a little, giggling as she clutched her tiny purse in her hand. "Your dress is beautiful," he said.

"Thank you. Nika sent it to me from Paris for my birthday."

"She always did have great taste; I'll give her that," he said, somewhat monotone.

Alexis just smiled, shaking her head as she walked out of the house, waiting while Sebastian closed the door behind them. He was not a fan of Nika. He never understood how two people who were so completely different could be best friends. Alexis had tried to explain to him how the difference in their personalities complemented one another; still, he was mystified by their closeness. Taking her hand, Sebastian led her down the front path. She glanced over his shoulder but didn't see his car anywhere. He smiled, gesturing to the street, where a limousine waited for them.

"I thought we would go in style tonight," he stated.

"This is turning out to be the best birthday ever."

He led her to the vehicle, where the driver stood beside the passenger door to open it for them. Alexis slid across the seat, and Sebastian slid in next to her. Inside, she noticed how plush the interior was, with a bottle of champagne waiting for them.

"Sebastian, you have outdone yourself," she beamed.

"I aim to please, my lady," he said, handing her a glass of champagne. They clinked their glasses together and took a sip.

"So, where are we going for dinner?" she asked.

"It's a secret, but I know you've always wanted to go there," he stated.

"Can I have a clue?"

"Nope, you just need to sit back and enjoy yourself," he said, a mischievous smile dancing across his handsome face.

Alexis did just that, enjoying the smooth ride. Classical music played softly in the background. The temperature in the limo was perfect, and the glass partition between them and the driver was all the way up, offering them complete privacy.

"So, how was your spa day?" Sebastian asked.

"It was so relaxing and rejuvenating, thank you."

"You're very welcome. I just wanted to make this birthday as special as possible for you. I love you."

Alexis stared deeply into his eyes. "I love you too." She leaned over to kiss him, and Sebastian swiftly pulled her onto his lap, causing her to laugh out loud. She paused just long enough for his lips to capture hers for a slow, deep kiss, the kind that always made her toes curl. She let out a sigh, sliding off his lap as the car began to slow. The car stopped and the driver opened the door for her. She stepped out and saw they were at Daniel's Broiler on Lake Union.

"You *are* sneaky, Mr. Kincaid," she said, hugging him.

"I knew you always wanted to come here, and I figured this was probably the best time," he replied. He offered his arm to escort her into the restaurant. "Shall we?"

Without a word, she took his arm, and together they walked towards the front door. Once inside, the maître d' greeted them, quickly showing them to their table. The table was beautifully set with a bottle of champagne chilled and ready, and there was a perfect view of the water. Sebastian helped Alexis into her chair, giving the waiter a nod to fill their glasses.

"I see you and the waiter are working together." She raised her glass to make a toast. "To the best boyfriend in the world. Thank you for making this birthday so incredible for me."

"You're welcome." He raised his glass to meet hers. He took a sip and set his glass down. "Did you ever think when we met all those years ago in California, you and I would be sitting in a restaurant like this celebrating your twenty-first birthday?"

Smiling, she sighed. "Never in my wildest dreams."

"I will do my best to make all your dreams come true tonight," he said, winking at her, a huge grin on his face.

She giggled, blushing a bit. "Then I will hold you to that later, Mr. Kincaid," she said coyly. "In the meantime, I think we should order some food because all this champagne is really starting to make me feel silly, and I think it would be terribly embarrassing to show up at the gallery opening drunk."

He laughed. "You're probably right. I hope you don't mind, but I took the liberty of ordering for us."

"Show-off," she replied with a wink.

He looked across the room and gave a nod. The maître d' appeared by her side again, this time carrying a silver dome-covered tray. He set it down in front of her, lifting the top to reveal a blue velvet box with a gold herringbone bracelet inside. The bracelet had a topaz in between two diamonds, a perfect complement to the locket she was wearing. It was gorgeous!

"Oh, Sebastian, it's beautiful."

Sebastian helped her put it on, admiring her smile and the sparkle in her eyes.

Their salads were placed in front of them, and shortly after they were done with them, the waitstaff came by to clear their plates. The waiter appeared with their main course, and Sebastian had selected the best of the best. Lobster.

They ate their dinner, talking about different things: family, school, and the future. They reminisced more about their childhoods, when both families were living in California in the small town of Paradise, located about eighty-five miles north of Sacramento. She and Sebastian grew up playing together, running up and down Stark Lane, a location she later learned was used for several scenes in one of her favorite movies. Alexis couldn't remember being happier than this evening with the man of her dreams, looking out at all the lights on Lake Union.

They finished their dinner and Sebastian paid the check. They walked out to the limousine, and Sebastian gave the driver directions to the gallery before joining Alexis in the backseat. He shifted in his seat to look at her. She kissed him softly, laying her head on his shoulder as they drove towards the gallery.

They pulled up to the gallery, and Alexis couldn't wait to go inside and see everything, especially the pieces she heard were rumored to be from Aidan's private collection. Sebastian gave both their names at the door, and they walked in. Alexis was overwhelmed with excitement, looking around to take it all in.

"Good evening," Aidan said. "I'm so glad you could make it. How was your dinner?"

"It was wonderful, and so was the company," Alexis said, slipping her arm through Sebastian's and gazing up at him.

"Delighted to hear it," Aidan replied. "Now, I know you want to see everything in the gallery."

"Definitely," she said with enthusiasm. "I'm also extremely interested in seeing anything from your private collection."

"Oh yes, my dear," Aidan replied. "All in good time. For now, why don't the two of you start in the Impressionist section? It's located just around the corner to the left," he said, gesturing with his arm.

They headed down the hall and around the corner, and Alexis was a captive audience with the pieces on display. She enjoyed Impressionism . . . Monet, Renoir, Manet, and then she stopped dead in her tracks, a slight gasp escaping her parted lips. There it was, her favorite. *A Sunday Afternoon on the Island of La Grande Jatte* by Seurat. She stared at the painting, mesmerized by the technique used to create such a masterpiece.

"I'm going to find the men's room," Sebastian whispered in her ear. "You good?"

"I'm good. I'm *so* good," she replied.

He chuckled a bit as he walked away. He loved her passion. Her eyes were affixed on the painting in front of her, studying all the colors. She took a step closer, engrossed in the beauty before her, not knowing she was also being studied.

"You seem quite taken with this one," Aidan said.

"I am," she replied. "I've always loved the idea of a million tiny dots making up something so massive." She took another step closer, then stepped back, her smile broader than before. "This is a wonderful copy."

He laughed. "You *do* know your history. How did you know?"

"The lighter border he added later," she said with confidence. She was happy she could impress him.

"Miss Alexis, I wonder if you would be interested in seeing the rest of my private collection," he said. "It is not something I normally do, but you have such a keen eye and a passion for art that I really admire."

She turned, staring at him, overwhelmed by the offer. "I would be honored, thank you, Mr. Drake."

He smiled. "Please, call me Aidan. The collection is at my home."

She hesitated for a moment, finding it a bit strange he would simply extend an invitation to her since they just met. "That's very generous of you but—" She glanced over her shoulder. *Where is Sebastian?* "Can I think about it?"

"Yes," he said with a smile. "In the meantime, I will be out of town for a few days to pick up a new piece for one of my collections. I will return in a week or so." Aidan noticed Sebastian approaching, and he already knew the young man didn't care for him. "I must go now and attend to the other guests. You enjoy the rest of the gallery."

"I will, thank you," she replied, watching him walk away.

"What was that about?" Sebastian asked.

"What do you mean?" she asked.

"Alexis, I see the way he looks at you. There's something about him I don't like, or more specifically, don't trust."

"We were just talking about art and his private collection, that's all." She studied his face for a moment. "Shall we go?"

"Are you sure? We haven't seen everything."

"I can come back another time," she stated. "The gallery isn't going anywhere, and it's close to home." As she moved her body into his, Sebastian leaned down, kissing her on the forehead. He took her hand as they walked towards the door. She decided not to tell him about the personal invitation to see the rest of Aidan's collection, especially since he didn't seem to trust Aidan.

It was a short drive from the gallery to her house, but when the limousine pulled up, a police car was waiting for them.

CHAPTER 9

Sebastian and Alexis got out of the limousine quickly, looking around for a sign of what had happened.

An officer approached them. "Alexis McBain?"

"Yes," she replied. "What's going on?"

"Do you know a Charlotte McCree?"

"She's my grandmother."

"I'm sorry to have to tell you this, but your grandmother was found last night just outside a small diner in Oregon," the officer stated.

"Is she okay?" Alexis asked, somehow already knowing the answer.

"No, I'm sorry to say she's not. She's dead," he replied.

Alexis had no words. It was as if she were suddenly being pulled down and sideways at the same time, the space around her closing in.

Sebastian put his arm around her to steady her. "Alexis let's go inside," he said softly, gently moving her forward, the police officer following. Sebastian retrieved the house key from her and opened the door. Inside, he led her over to the sofa, sitting her down. "I'll be right back." He headed into the kitchen and returned with a glass of water, handing it to her. She mindlessly accepted the glass, holding it in her lap.

The officer sat in the side chair across from her, and Sebastian joined her on the sofa. "I'm very sorry for your loss, Miss McBain."

"What happened?" she asked as silent tears began to fall.

"It looked like she had a stroke or something," the officer stated. "Do you know where she was going?"

"She was driving down to Portland for a few days to meet with some old friends. She must have stopped for a bite or maybe to grab some coffee." Alexis stared in the direction of the officer, not making eye contact.

"We found her car parked in front of a diner, and her keys were locked inside the car." He paused for a moment before he continued. "She was actually found around the corner in the alley next to the diner."

"What?" she asked. "That makes no sense. Why would she be in the alley, and why would her keys be locked in her car?"

"Perhaps she became confused after she locked her keys in the car," the officer stated. "Did your grandmother have any health issues at all?"

"No, my grandmother was in perfect health," she replied defensively. Sebastian placed his right hand on the small of her back, attempting to soothe her.

"I'm sorry, Miss McBain. My intention was not to upset you any more than you already are."

"I know," she said quietly. "I'm sorry. It just doesn't make any sense."

"She will be transported back to Seattle tomorrow, and arrangements have already been made for her car to be returned to you," the officer explained.

"Thank you," she said, taking a sip of water. "Wait, I'm sorry. Who made the arrangements?"

"We found a card in your grandmother's wallet with instructions to contact you and her lawyer should anything happen to her. I'm told Mr. Blake will be in calling you within a day or two."

"Thank you, Officer," Sebastian said, standing. The officer stood, and Sebastian walked him to the front door. He closed the door behind the man and walked back to the sofa. Alexis sat there, glass of water still in her hand, her eyes affixed on nothing. He sat next to her but did not speak, partly because he wasn't sure what to say. He reached over, taking the glass from her hand, and set it on the coffee table. Then he sat back, gently pulling Alexis towards him. Her head fell to the comfort of his chest, and he held her as she cried.

They sat together until Alexis was quiet and Sebastian could tell from her breathing that she was asleep. Carefully, he scooped her up, carrying her upstairs to her room. He laid her down on the bed, slipping her shoes off. He removed his shoes, shirt, and tie before climbing in next to her, wrapping his arms around her. He wasn't sure what tomorrow would bring, but tonight, they both needed sleep. She would stir now and then, silent tears falling as she slept, and he would gently stroke her hair until the fitful stirring passed. Then he slept.

CHAPTER 10

Paris, France

It was Nika's last night in Paris, and she was determined to have a good time. She headed out to a nightclub, different from the last one. *He* had told her to never hunt in the same place twice. She needed to keep a low profile, which was a lot to ask of her. After all, when Nika went out, she wanted to be seen. *What's the point otherwise?*

She entered the club, the music blasting some dance remix of ABC's "Poison Arrow." There were bodies everywhere and emotions were running high. As soon as she entered the crowd, her hunger took hold. She really needed to learn to control it better. It had only been a few months since the change. She focused on the music until she regained her composure. Moving through the crowd, quickly making her way past the bar to the dance floor, she paused briefly when she noticed the most beautiful piercing blue eyes she had ever seen.

He was standing at the bar with a couple of friends, but he might as well have been standing alone, as everyone else seemed to fade away. He was tall, over six feet, with dark wavy hair that was a bit longer in the back. He wore all black, and his shirt had three buttons undone. She noticed a dark patch of hair sprawled across his pale skin. *What a beautiful contrast.* As the colored lights changed, igniting all the corners of the room, his eyes seemed to absorb some of those colors, and they danced.

As soon as she reached the dance floor, Nika started to move with the music. She danced around to face his direction, their eyes meeting again. She smiled at him, and he smiled back. He quickly excused himself, looking her over from head to toe as he approached. She was wearing a short royal-blue dress that came just above her knees. It hugged her body, showing off every curve she had, and it had an open back to display a little of her perfect porcelain skin. Black heels completed her outfit.

He smiled at her when he got to the dance floor, moving with her to the rhythm of the music. He knew how to dance, and that impressed her. They stared into each other's eyes, and when the music changed to a slower song, she stepped forward towards the man. He wrapped his arms around her waist and pulled her close to his body. She placed her hands on his chest, sliding them up so her arms could encircle his neck. She gazed into those gorgeous blue eyes and smiled.

"Hi," she said.

"Hello there. My name is Dash. What's yours?"

"Nika."

"I'm sure you must hear this all the time, but you are beautiful."

"Thank you so much."

"Are you here with anyone?"

She let her eyes fall away for a moment. "I'm here with you, but I wasn't planning on staying long."

His head fell back as he let out a chuckle, a huge smile on his face. "Was there somewhere else you would rather be?"

An undeniable look of lust appeared on her face. "Wherever you think is best."

"I've got just the place," he said. He took one of her hands, leading her off the dance floor, tossing a nod towards his friends as he led Nika out of the club.

They hailed a taxi, and ten minutes later they were at his flat, which seemed to resemble so many she had seen in the last couple of months, no concept of design or taste. Dash led her straight to his bedroom. He kissed her passionately, and she could tell he was experienced. She had to control herself because all she wanted to do was taste him, and she knew if she gave him a chance, he would be able to satisfy her other needs. It *had* been a while. He reached down and grabbed her legs, pulling her up so they could encircle his waist. She wrapped her arms around his neck as they continued kissing. He caressed her left leg, his hand traveling further up her thigh to cup her buttocks, only to discover she was not wearing anything under her dress.

He pulled back from the kiss, a knowing grin on his face. "You're just full of surprises, aren't you?"

She laughed out loud. "You'll see." She unwrapped her legs from his waist, sliding down the length of his body. He *was* tall. She took a step back, watching his face as she carefully slipped the top of the dress down over her shoulders. She pulled her arms out of the long sleeves, rolling the dress down to her waist, arching her back and pushing her bare breasts high into the air. She paused for a moment, watching as he began unbuttoning his own shirt, tossing it aside. When he reached for the button on his pants, she smiled, teasing a little more as she turned away from him slightly before sliding her dress over her hips, again arching her back and pushing her little round ass towards him. When the dress hit the floor, Nika kicked it over to the corner with the toe of her shoe, turning slowly to face him. Dash was captivated as he slid out of his pants, slipping his shoes off at the same time, watching her hands caress her perfect skin, down her flat stomach, up and over the curve of her hips. She stepped forward, and he grabbed her around the waist. He pulled her in for a kiss, holding her body close while he reclined back on the bed. She fell forward on top of him, wasting no time.

Ready for him, she leaned forward a little, pushing the toe of her shoes into the mattress and maneuvering into position before sitting back, slowly allowing all of him to be engulfed inside her. His head fell back, and a deep moan escaped his lips. She sat there for a moment, watching his face as her muscles slowly squeezed around him.

"Oh my God!" he exclaimed, just above a whisper.

Nika could feel her own excitement rising, and she knew her eyes and teeth would change soon. *Time to pick up the pace*. She leaned back further, placing her hands behind her on his thighs, his muscles rigid beneath her open palms. Warm hands encircled her firm breasts as he gently squeezed them, flicking his thumb across the hardened nipples. She moaned loudly, knowing it was time. Dash was almost there, his breathing and moans coming faster. As he discharged his remaining energy into her, she pitched her body forward, sinking her fangs into the right side of his neck as she continued grinding her pelvis against him, with him still deep inside her. Swallowing the last of his blood, she reached her own peak, pulling back and crying out with pleasure as her entire body quivered.

Regaining her composure, she slowed her movements and opened her eyes to gaze down at the strong body beneath her. His lips were parted, and his eyes were frozen half shut, allowing her one last glimpse of their crystal blue color. *Such a shame*, she thought. *I really would have enjoyed keeping him around.*

She walked to the bathroom to grab a quick shower. She had enjoyed Paris and everything it had offered her over the last couple of months, but she was ready to get back to Seattle. *He* would be arriving the next day, and she still had some packing to do.

Finishing her shower, Nika wandered back into the bedroom. She looked back at the lifeless body lying on the bed and wondered if she should have taken more time with him. *Oh well. Too late now.*

She slipped back into her dress and put her shoes on before heading out the door. Tomorrow was going to be a busy day.

CHAPTER 11

Seattle

The smell of coffee made everything seem right until Alexis remembered. She turned to see Sebastian lying in bed with her, both still wearing their clothes from the previous night. He was still asleep, but he must have gotten up at some point to start the coffee. He knew her so well.

She quietly crawled out of bed so as not to disturb him, walking down the hall to the bathroom without bothering to turn on any lights. The dim light coming in through the window was all she could stand, her eyes heavy and red from last night's tears. She turned the water on and started to undress, laying her clothes across the countertop. She carefully removed the necklace and the rest of her jewelry, setting them down on top of her clothes. She stepped into the shower, the warm water having little effect on her. It felt good but she was cold, colder than she should have been. She reached for the control valve, increasing the heat, steam filling the space around her. She leaned against wall, and the cold tile sent a sharper chill through her. The warm steam paled compared to the hot tears falling as she stared at the corner of the wall.

She had no idea how long she had been crying when she felt his arms wrap around her from behind. He rested his chin on top of her left shoulder, the side of his face pressed gently against hers. He didn't say anything, he didn't have to. His arms around her were enough to comfort her. *What would I do without him?*

The sudden decrease in the temperature caused Sebastian to reach past Alexis to turn the water off. He pulled the curtain back and reached for a towel to wrap around his waist. He stepped out of the shower, retrieving a towel for her. Mindlessly, she stepped out, and he wrapped a towel around her body, blotting her dry before grabbing her robe from the back of the bathroom door. They walked down the hall to her room, and Sebastian put on some sweats he had left there a few weeks before.

"Hungry?" he asked her.

"Not really," she replied, her eyes cast down.

"How about some coffee?"

"Okay."

They walked downstairs to the kitchen, and she sat at the breakfast table while he poured them both a cup of coffee. He walked over, setting a coffee cup in front of her before taking a seat himself. She picked up the cup and held it with both hands, staring out in front of her. She finally took a sip and looked over at him. He smiled, and she managed a smile back.

They finished their coffee sitting in silence. Alexis stood and walked into the living room, taking a seat on the far end of the sofa. She tucked her legs underneath her and stared out the window. Sebastian walked over to the sofa, taking a seat at the opposite end. He knew she was hurting, but he didn't want to crowd her.

"Is there anything I can do for you?"

"No," she replied, staring out the window. "I think I just need to be alone. I might just go back to bed."

"I understand," he said. "I'll come by later this evening with some dinner, if you like."

"Thank you," she said. She looked at him for a moment before she stood. He followed her to the front door and when she opened it, she realized his car was not outside. The limousine had dropped them off last night. She turned, picking up her keys to hand them to him. "You don't have a car, so just take mine. I can't imagine I'll need to go anywhere today."

"Thank you," he said, taking the keys and gently brushing his lips against hers. "I'll be back a little later."

"Okay," she said. She smiled as he stepped out the door. "Thank you again, Sebastian."

"I love you," he said softly.

"I love you too."

She watched him walk to her car and get in before closing the door. Wandering back into the living room, the grandfather clock started to chime. It was nine a.m., and she felt exhausted. Walking back upstairs, she stopped by the bathroom to get the locket. She put it on, and when the locket touched her skin, she felt a familiar comfort come over her. It was all she had left of her family now. She walked into her bedroom, crawled back into bed, and pulled the covers up over her head. She exhaled one last time before closing her eyes and drifting off to sleep.

CHAPTER 12

Alexis slept all day, finally waking to notice the sun was setting. She climbed out of bed, changing out of her robe and into some sweatpants and a sweatshirt, adding fuzzy slippers for comfort. She brushed her hair, pulled it back into a ponytail, and washed her face. Walking downstairs, she turned on a lamp, jumping slightly when she heard a knock at the door. Through the peephole she saw Sebastian and Josh outside. Opening the door, she was greeted by the wonderful smell of Chinese food, her favorite. There were a few bags between the two of them.

"How much food did you bring?" she asked.

"Plenty," Sebastian replied with a big smile. Josh just shook his head, laughing at his friend.

"Thank you, guys. You can put it in the kitchen." She stepped back to let them in. Sebastian led the way with Josh and Alexis following. They set the bags of food down on the counter while Alexis got some plates from the cabinet. They all dished out what they wanted and sat down at the table in the breakfast area. After setting her plate down, Alexis grabbed some beer for the guys and poured a glass of wine for herself. They ate, talking about random things: the change in the weather, how the football season was shaping up so far, nothing too heavy. After they finished, Sebastian gathered their plates, rinsed them off, and put them in the dishwasher.

Alexis stood and walked into the living room, and the guys followed. She and Sebastian sat on the sofa, and Josh sat in one of the side chairs.

"Thanks again for bringing the food," she said. "It was really good."

"You're welcome," Josh replied. "You looked like you hadn't eaten all day by the way you went after it," he teased.

"No, I hadn't," she said, smiling.

"There are enough leftovers if you get hungry later," Sebastian said. "Do you want to watch a movie or something?"

"No," she replied. "I think I need to get ready for my meeting with the lawyer."

"Okay," Sebastian said. "I think we're gonna go, but you call me if you need anything."

"I will," she said. "I promise."

She walked them to the door, and Josh headed out first to start the car.

Sebastian studied her beautiful face for a moment, leaning in to kiss her softly.

"Your car keys," he said, removing them from his pocket.

"Thanks," she said.

He turned and jogged over to join Josh in his car, and she stood in the doorway, watching as the taillights disappeared into the night before closing the door.

She walked down the hall into her grandmother's study. It felt odd being in the study by herself. She sat down at the desk and turned the lamp on so she could see. She noticed the calendar with some appointments here and there, realizing there were a few calls she would need to make over the next couple of days. Opening the lower drawer on the right side of the desk, she removed all her grandmother's important files: for the house, the cars, and insurance information. She looked everything over briefly, also grabbing a notepad to make a few notes and questions she might have.

When she was done, she gathered all the files and notes, turning the light off before walking out of the study. She entered the kitchen and set everything down on the table. She looked at the clock above the phone hanging on the wall. It was almost eight p.m. She had no idea she was in the study that long. Sighing, she walked over to the counter and poured herself a glass of wine. She flipped the light on for the range hood before turning the overhead light off in the kitchen. Looking around the room in the dim light, a flood of memories came back to her. So much time spent in the kitchen either watching Gram bake an amazing dessert or helping her prepare a meal. She sighed again before picking up her glass of wine and walking into the living room. She set her glass down on the coffee table and walked over to the stereo. She looked through a few of her grandmother's albums, finally pulling one of the records out of its cover and placing it on the turntable. She clicked the switch to make it play a specific song, a favorite of her grandmother's.

Alexis turned the lamp off on her way over to the sofa, sitting down just as the music filled the darkness. Nina Simone, "Who Knows Where the Time Goes." She picked up her glass of wine, repositioning herself sideways on the sofa. She stretched her legs out in front of her, leaned back against the arm behind her, and closed her eyes as Nina sang to her. She knew exactly how she felt. She sipped her wine, smiling as she remembered what an incredible woman her grandmother was. She had taught her so much.

There were a few tears, but they were different from the previous tears she had shed. The locket felt warm against her skin, and a sense of calm increased inside her as the music played, almost as if her grandmother were there with her.

She finished her wine, setting her glass down on the floor before pulling a throw blanket down over her legs. Gram had blankets all over the house it seemed, just in case you got cold. She smiled, realizing she was going to be experiencing memories like this for a while. Everywhere she looked in the house, a little piece of her grandmother reminded her of all the years they shared together. Pressing the side of her body into the back of the sofa, she closed her eyes as Nina sang her to sleep.

CHAPTER 13

Alexis woke the next morning with a sense of peace that could not be explained lingering in the air. She glanced at the grandfather clock to see it was just before seven a.m., and the sun was rising. She threw the blanket back from her legs and dropped her feet down to the floor, rolling her toes over to stretch the tops of her feet. Just another habit left over from dance training. Standing, she stretched, looking around the room. It was a bit chilly, so she adjusted the thermostat on the wall, also turning off the power to the stereo. The lawyer's office would not open for a few hours, so she headed into the kitchen for some coffee and breakfast.

Everything still felt surreal to her, but she knew she had to move forward. She poured a cup of coffee, putting it in the micro-wave to heat it up. She decided to have a piece of toast with peanut butter on it with a banana. After she ate, she went upstairs to figure out what she was going to wear. She selected a black long-sleeved blouse, her gray pencil skirt that came just below her knees, and tall black leather boots. It was getting colder outside.

After laying her clothes out, she walked into the bathroom. She stared in the mirror for a moment, disappointed at the reflection looking back at her. It was going to take a little more effort than usual to make herself presentable. She showered quickly and was drying off when she heard the phone ring. She picked up the extension in her room. It was the lawyer's secretary calling to let her know Mr. Blake would be available for a meeting that morning around ten a.m. Alexis confirmed she would be there and hung up. It was just before eight. She walked back into the bathroom to do her hair and makeup.

Finally satisfied with the face in the mirror, she walked into her room and got dressed. She headed downstairs to find her purse. The previous days were a bit of a blur, and she couldn't remember where she had left it. She finally found it next to her book bag. Book bag. School. She was already well into the quarter, but Alexis no longer felt up to it. Something to add to her to-do list. She removed the books and notebook from the bag, walking into the kitchen to put all the records she had pulled from the study into it. She looked at the clock on the wall above the phone. It was 9:15 a.m. She would have plenty of time to get to the building downtown. The lawyer's secretary had given her the address and directions. Still, she would be driving in Monday morning traffic. She decided to get a move on.

She arrived at the lawyer's office just before ten a.m., taking a seat in the reception area. At 10:01 a.m., the lawyer appeared.

"Good morning, Miss McBain. I'm Mr. Blake," he said, extending his hand. Alexis stood to shake his hand. "Please come in." He gestured to his office just across from where she was sitting. "Louise, please hold my calls," he said to the secretary.

His office had a warm feeling to it, with wood paneling on the walls and several bookshelves filled with books. His law degree and other accomplishments were hanging on the opposite wall, flanked by a few art pieces. A large mahogany desk with a black leather chair behind it sat in the center of the room. Alexis walked over to the window, taking in the view of the city below. Cars and people scurried about, starting their day full of energy and enthusiasm. *Ah, to be one of them.*

Alexis heard the door close and glanced behind her to see Mr. Blake studying her as he walked across the room.

"First, I would like to express my deepest condolences for the loss of your grandmother," he said, extending his hands to hers. "Charlotte was a very sweet woman, and she will be missed."

"Thank you, Mr. Blake," she said, taking his hands and smiling when he gave them a gentle squeeze. "I want to thank you for any assistance you can offer me."

"I am here for anything and everything you need," he said as he gestured towards the chairs across from his desk. "Please, have a seat and we can get started."

Alexis walked over and sat down in a chair, pulling out all the files she had brought with her and placing them in her lap. "I've brought everything Gram had on the house, cars, and insurance. I hope I didn't forget anything," she said. "I also made a list of questions."

Mr. Blake smiled, sitting across from her. "It must run in the family."

"What must run in the family?" she asked, feeling slightly perplexed.

"Being prepared," he said. "Your grandmother would be proud. She made arrangements so you wouldn't have to worry about a thing. This should explain everything." He pulled an envelope out from a folder in front of him, handing it to Alexis. "Your grandmother wanted me to give this to you."

She took the sealed envelope from him and opened it to read the contents.

Alexis,

If you are reading this letter, it is because I am no longer with you, and for that, I am sorry, my dear girl. I have made sure you will have everything you need to move forward with your life financially. My lawyer has instructions to assist you with everything. The house now belongs to you, as does everything in it. I have planned for you to receive part of your inheritance now, to help you complete your schooling or for whatever you need, and you will receive the rest when you turn 25 years old.

I am sorry I left you so suddenly, but I know you will be okay. You are strong and come from good stock. Please remember, I will always be with you, just as your parents are.

Love Always,
Gram

Tears welled up in her eyes as she finished reading the letter, and as if on cue, Mr. Blake handed her a tissue.

"Thank you," she said, accepting it and blotting her eyes. "I'm sorry, I really hate crying in front of people, especially people I don't know."

"No need to apologize," he said. "It's quite understandable."

"Thank you. Gram said in the letter that everything was taken care of, financially speaking, and she also mentioned an inheritance?"

Mr. Blake nodded, turning the file in front of him around so Alexis could see the contents. There were several documents inside, all with an *X* somewhere, indicating a signature was required.

"These are the documents Ms. McCree had drawn up to transfer all of her personal property and any other business holdings into your name. She was quite specific about everything, including how much of your inheritance you will receive now."

"I'm confused," Alexis stated, blotting her nose. "What do you mean business holdings?"

"Ms. McCree was quite a savvy businesswoman. She had several stock investments in some fairly new companies, mostly those she felt would grow and become extremely profitable in the future," he explained. "As I said, your grandmother was a very savvy businesswoman."

Alexis could hardly believe what she was hearing. *Gram, a savvy businesswoman?* It seemed like he was talking about someone else. Gram was the woman who loved gardening and baking. She loved searching for new antiques for the house. She shook her head in disbelief.

"Is something wrong?" he asked.

"No," she replied. "It just sounds like I didn't really know my grandmother."

"She spoke of you often, and she wanted to make sure you wouldn't have anything to worry about," he stated. "That's why I am at your disposal."

"I really do appreciate that, Mr. Blake. Thank you."

He smiled at her, and she managed a smile back. "The funeral is scheduled for this coming Wednesday at one p.m., and all the necessary calls have already been made."

"Okay," she responded in a quiet voice, her mind trying to sort through everything she had just heard. It felt like he was speaking a foreign language, so much information coming at her about things she knew nothing about.

He removed one of the gold pens from his desk set and laid it on top of the papers in front of her. "I just need to get your signature on a few documents, and then the financial transfers can be completed."

Alexis picked up the pen, reading each document carefully before signing it, one of the many things her grandmother had taught her. Mr. Blake explained things that were not obvious, pointing out the different stocks that now belonged to her in the stock portfolio. He also reviewed the house and property taxes as well as what her options would be if she ever decided to sell the house. Once everything was signed, they both stood, and she followed him to the door.

"Thank you again for all your help today," she said.

"You are most welcome, Alexis," he replied, with a handshake. "Please call me if you have any questions in the future."

Once the door to his office was closed, Mr. Blake walked back to his desk and dialed a number. "It's done," he said into the receiver and hung up. He wasn't sure what was going to happen with Alexis McBain at this point, but at least he knew *he* and *his family* were going to be safe.

Alexis left the office building, her mind still trying to understand everything she had signed and all the financial changes, like the new balance in her bank accounts, plus all the new stock she had acquired. None of it seemed to matter though because she just wanted Gram back. Pulling out of the parking lot into traffic, she decided to move forward with some other business. She drove to school and filled out the necessary paperwork to withdraw from her classes. She needed to figure out what she was going to do next, and she needed time to think. She decided to stop by the gym on the way home, knowing Sebastian would be there. When she got there, she looked around the gym, walking back to the business office where she found the guys talking.

"Hey there," Sebastian said, standing up to offer her his chair. He stepped back, leaning against the wall while Josh quietly watched her, his poker face firmly in place.

She sat down and exhaled before speaking. "I saw the lawyer this morning and signed everything," she announced. "I also stopped by school and withdrew from all my classes."

"Are you sure about that, dropping out of school?" Sebastian walked towards her, sitting on the front edge of the desk.

"I just need to figure some things out," she said. "I don't feel like I would be able to concentrate on school right now."

"Okay," Sebastian said, his tone soothing. "Whatever you need."

"I think I just need to go home." She was tired.

"Would you like some company?" Sebastian asked.

"No, I need to be alone," she stated. "I *am* concerned about Nika though."

Sebastian looked perplexed. "What do you mean?"

"She was supposed to come home yesterday, and I haven't heard from her," she said. "I called and left a message at her aunt's house, but I never heard back. I just hope she's okay."

"I'm sure Nika is fine," Sebastian said. "She's good at taking care of herself."

Alexis was suddenly on her feet and heading for the door. Josh sat there, confused in silence, watching Sebastian follow Alexis.

"Hey, I'm sorry."

Alexis turned and looked at Sebastian. "I am genuinely concerned about my friend, and I miss her."

"I know," Sebastian said, stepping closer to offer her an embrace. She wrapped her arms around his waist, pressing her head against his firm chest. "She's probably tired from her travels. I'm sure she'll call you in the next day or two."

Alexis held on to Sebastian. "I know she's not your favorite person," she said, pulling back to look up at his face, "but she is still my best friend. I just need to know that she's all right."

"And I'm sure you will know in a day or so."

"You're probably right," she replied. "I'm just tired and . . ."

"And what?" he asked, caressing her face as she looked down.

She looked up at him, and her eyes were brimming with unshed tears. "I just feel so overwhelmed and lost, I guess," she finally said.

"That is completely understandable," he said, kissing her forehead. He could tell she was fighting to keep from falling apart. "Are you sure you're okay to drive right now?"

"Yeah, I just, oh God, Josh." She pulled back, looking over at him, realizing he was still in the room. "I'm so sorry." She brushed the tears away from her face. This was becoming a bad habit, crying in front of people.

Josh stood up and walked over to her to give her a hug. "It's cool. There's no need to apologize." He released her, gesturing towards the small bedroom through a door behind the office. "Why don't you splash some water on your face, take a moment?"

"I will, thank you," she said, walking past him through the doorway of the bedroom and closing the door behind her.

Josh turned and looked at Sebastian, completely confused. "What the hell was that about?" His tone was hushed.

Sebastian just shook his head. "She and Nika have been friends for like, forever," he began. "They are as different as night and day, and I don't think Nika has ever really cared about Alexis or her feelings, but Alexis can be very protective of her, saying she's just misunderstood."

"Okay," Josh said. "Well, thank you for never introducing me to *that* mess."

"Oh, trust me, man," Sebastian began with a chuckle. "She wouldn't look twice at you. She'd feel you were beneath her."

"Yeah, well some chicks are just slow," Josh said with a hint of arrogance.

Sebastian laughed, punching his friend in the arm.

Alexis came out of the bathroom looking more like herself. She thanked both again and left the gym. She drove home, unsure what she was going to do once she got there. She went upstairs and changed her clothes before coming back down to make a cup of coffee. She wasn't hungry, so she decided to go into the den to see what old movies were on TV. She grabbed a blanket from the trunk nearby and curled up in her grandmother's favorite big chair. She flipped through a few channels until she found a movie to watch, a musical. She sipped on her coffee as the infectious tunes carried her away for a while.

CHAPTER 14

Alexis closed the front door and leaned against it, feeling emotionally wrung out. The service was beautiful, and it was so nice of Sebastian's parents to host the gathering afterward at their house. Gram really *had* taken care of everything. Alexis was deeply moved by the number of people who came to pay their respects. Her grandmother was a remarkable woman who touched so many lives.

She was glad to be home, but the house that had always felt so warm and inviting, with comfortable furniture and the warm tones of the hardwood floors, today felt colder than ever before. It had nothing to do with the temperature of the room and everything to do with her. Sebastian had offered to come home with her, concerned with how much time she was spending by herself. She loved him for caring so much but said no and apologized, feeling like she just wouldn't be particularly good company. He said he understood. He just wanted to give her whatever she needed. She still had not heard from Nika, which didn't help.

She had tried calling Nika's family, but they were all out of town. She just hoped her friend was okay. She missed her.

Alexis headed upstairs, walking down the hall past her room to her grandmother's room. She had not been in Gram's room since the night before she left for Oregon. Standing in the doorway, she exhaled the last of her hesitation and entered the room, walking past the bed and the old chest, over to the window to see a perfect view of the Space Needle. She remembered the first time Gram had taken her up to the restaurant in the Space Needle and the time they spent on the observation deck, looking out over the city. Alexis was only ten years old at the time, holding on to her grandmother's hand tightly as she ventured closer to the railing, looking down at all the people walking below. She asked her grandmother about the netting just below the observation level, learning about the few people who jumped from the deck. Alexis couldn't understand at the time why anybody would do that.

She closed her eyes for a moment, the memory lingering in the back of her mind. Alexis opened her eyes to see the city lights coming on and the lights on the Needle lighting up the sky. Staring out the window, she was surprised how different everything looked.

Turning to leave the room, she stopped in front of the chest, staring down at the massive lock hanging on the front. It had always been locked. She reached down with her left hand and pulled at the big lock, laughing a bit when it didn't give. *What was I thinking?* She released the lock from her hand, walking away when she heard a loud click resonate throughout the room after the lock hit the chest. She stared at it for a moment, slowly walking back over to the chest. She bent down to remove the lock. She was finally going to see inside after all these years. She dropped the lock onto the floor, jumping a little from the deep thud it made against the carpet. She carefully lifted the heavy lid up and rested it against the foot of the bed. It was incredibly dark inside. She leaned forward over the chest, placing her left hand on the back edge, trying to get a better look. Her thumb brushed against something along the back. It felt like a switch. She flipped the switch with her thumb, and the inside of the chest lit up, revealing a wooden ladder mounted against the wall directly below the left edge of the chest and a landing below the chest opening. She couldn't believe her eyes. It was a basement she never knew existed. How could there be a basement on the second floor of the house when the study was directly below her? She stood staring down into the space for a few minutes, debating whether she should call Sebastian or check it out herself.

Alexis slipped off her heels and her jacket before carefully swinging her right leg over the edge of the chest and stepping down to the third rung of the ladder while holding on to the sides. She pulled her left leg in and stepped down to the next rung. The ladder was sturdy as she carefully climbed down to the landing, her locket bouncing back and forth against her chest. She noticed a pulley system mounted on the wall to the right of the ladder with a metal basket attached to it. Turning slowly, she walked away from the ladder, pausing when she saw the enclosed stairs lit halfway down with handrails attached to the walls.

Holding on to the railing, Alexis walked down the stairs, her mind racing, wondering what she might find at the bottom. She looked around in the dimly lit space, trying to make out what was down there. Glancing to the right in the darkened space, she discovered a small round table with a candle on it and matches. She struck a match and lit the candle, then turned to see the rest of the room. Walking over to a long table on the outside wall, she found more candles, as well as some bowls and jars, varying in size. She struck another match and lit the candle closest to her on the table and watched as all the candles ignited. She took a step back. *How is that possible? How is this place possible?* She looked around the room again. There had to be a light switch somewhere. Walking back over to the small table at the bottom of the stairs, she ran her hand along the wall and flipped the switch, filling the basement with light.

Alexis couldn't believe her eyes. She looked around the room and saw the wall to the left of the small table was full of wine. There had to be close to a hundred bottles of wine on the wall. She chuckled, remembering a counting song from her childhood. Walking along the wall, she reached out with her fingertips, touching a bottle every few steps, noting all the different types of wine. Reds, whites, and some blends. No wonder there was always wine in the house, because there was *always* wine in the house. Across from the wall of wine, there were bookshelves full of books and a sitting area just a few feet in front of the shelves. Two oversized cozy chairs were on either side of a large round table, and there were several books sitting on top. Her breath caught in her throat when Alexis saw a white envelope with her name on it on top of the stack of books, written in Gram's handwriting. She sat down in one of the chairs and opened the envelope to read the letter.

Alexis,

I am sorry I cannot be there with you to show you who you are and from where you came. It started many years ago with our ancestors.

You come from a long line of natural healers, something that is part of the bloodline for all the females in our family, in our coven. We are healers and protectors for those who cannot protect themselves. There are many evils in this world, and we are sworn to protect others against them. The tapestries on the wall with the different family crests show you who we are. We all work together.

You will find a hidden room under the stairs, where the most important books are located. All the information you need is there. I have also included the name of someone who can assist you with additional questions you may have, my dear friend Margaret. You probably met her at my funeral. She is waiting for your call.

It is also time for Sebastian to be made aware of everything. The two of you were meant for each other. Together, you and your children will continue what was started so many years ago.

The locket I gave you will help protect you against evil as it has for many in the past. It should be passed down to your daughter as it was passed down to me.

Please know this is not how I wanted to introduce you to your destiny; however, I know you will become everything you were meant to be and more. I am so proud of you, and I will always be with you.

Love Always,
Gram

Alexis was stunned, reaching up to caress the locket. It was almost more than she could wrap her mind around, yet it explained so much. Every time someone she cared about would get hurt, she always seemed to know how to help or what to do. Sebastian and others had always told her what a healing touch she had, and now she knew why. Glancing down at the locket in her hand, she watched as the center glowed, a small flare of light, and she finally understood. She looked over at the tapestries hanging along the far wall, reading the names out loud: McCree, McBain, and Kincaid. The names of her grandmother, her parents, and Sebastian and his family.

She stood up, still holding the letter, and walked over to the long table where all the candles were burning. They emitted so much warmth, and the flames danced now as she stood next to them, like they recognized who she was. The hidden room. She walked away from the table and around a corner to a set of bifold doors, opening them to find another bookshelf. The books were all leather bound and looked incredibly old. She needed more information. She looked down at the letter again, at the phone number for Margaret.

Alexis closed the closet doors and walked back over to the table of candles, leaning down to blow one out, amused as all were extinguished at the same time. She extinguished the candle on the small table before running up the stairs. She needed answers, she needed to make a call. She needed to know more before she brought Sebastian into it.

When she reached the top of the ladder, she carefully climbed out of the chest, something she never thought she would do. She closed the chest and picked the lock up off the floor. She wondered. She clamped the lock shut and then held it in her left hand. She looked at it for a moment before pulling on the lock with her right hand. It unlatched from the locked position. Good to know. She locked the chest again and then headed to her room. She quickly changed into jeans and a sweater. She sat down on her bed, dialing the number in the letter.

"Hello," a female voice said.

"Hello," Alexis said. "I'm looking for Margaret?"

"Alexis," the voice said. "It's Margaret. I've been waiting for your call."

"Can you come to my grand . . . my house?" she asked.

"Yes, I can," Margaret replied, her smile coming through the phone. "I will be there in twenty minutes."

CHAPTER 15

So many questions were racing through her mind, Alexis could hardly contain herself. She was sitting in the living room when she heard the knock on the front door. She moved quickly, peering through the peephole. True to her word, Margaret arrived at the house within twenty minutes. Alexis opened the door and was greeted by a sweet round-faced woman she remembered seeing at the funeral.

"Hello, Alexis," the woman said. "I'm Margaret. May I come in?"

"Of course," Alexis said, taking a step back, allowing the woman to enter. She walked in and headed directly into the living room as if she had been there many times before. Alexis closed the door and followed the woman. They both sat down on the sofa, Margaret rotating slightly to look at Alexis, her face serene.

"I imagine you have many questions, my dear, and I am here to help you find the answers," Margaret stated. She set her purse down on the sofa beside her, hands in her lap.

"First, I would like to thank you for coming," Alexis began.

"You are quite welcome," Margaret replied.

"I'm not even sure where to start," Alexis said. "Obviously, I found the basement and the letter, but where do I go from there and why didn't Gram tell me about this sooner? What am I, exactly?"

Margaret smiled before speaking. "You are from a long line of natural healers and protectors. To start, you can help heal people through touch."

"What do you mean, 'to start'?" Alexis asked.

"I know it's a lot to take in, and I promise to help you any way I can," Margaret stated.

"Okay, thank you," Alexis said. "Oh, I'm so sorry. Can I get you anything to drink?"

"A glass of water would be lovely, thank you."

Alexis went to the kitchen, returning with two glasses of water. She set them down on the coffee table, then sat back down on the sofa.

She looked at Margaret, who was taking a sip of her water. She set the glass down and smiled at Alexis. "Let me start with how you came to be," Margaret began. Alexis turned sideways on the sofa to get more comfortable. "It started many years ago when one of your great-aunts met a wonderfully charming and handsome man. He was everything she had hoped for, and the thought of spending the rest of her life with him filled her with happiness, but he was not what he claimed to be. He was pure evil. He was . . . a vampire."

"A what?" Alexis asked, chuckling a little.

"I know," Margaret said, nodding. "You had no idea they were real, but I can assure you, they are very real. Your great-aunt was killed by his lover, an incredibly dangerous vampire in her own right. He wanted to avenge her death, but the coven managed to drive him out of the area before anyone else could be harmed.

"Where did he go?" Alexis asked.

"They lost track of him, unfortunately, many years ago," Margaret said. "His name was Lorcan McCowan, but the coven has not been able to locate him in years."

"How old is he?" Alexis asked.

"He is well over four hundred years old," Margaret said, "but he appears to be no older than thirty-five."

Alexis sat for a moment, trying to wrap her mind around the bizarre information this woman was telling her. Never in her life did she think somebody would be telling her vampires were real. She had always enjoyed watching the movies of this genre and was fascinated with the whole concept, but real? No way. "So, did this *vampire* know the young woman was part of the coven?" Alexis asked.

"We believe he did," Margaret said. "He was just toying with her, taking his time. His lover was much more ruthless. We believe the young woman's purity was what drew his lover to her. His lover, Genevieve, was younger and had far less control over herself, but she knew your great-aunt was destined to become immensely powerful. They both feared she would be able to destroy them, and that is why Genevieve killed her."

"Okay," Alexis said, taking it all in. "Why did Gram wait to tell me about my abilities and where I came from?"

"Your grandmother was trying to protect you," Margaret said. "It is a fluke you are even still alive."

"What do you mean a *fluke*?" Alexis asked.

Margaret stared at her for a moment, and Alexis could sense there was something she needed to tell her but was afraid to share. Alexis sat, patiently waiting. "You were six years old, and you and Gram drove up to Seattle before your parents, remember?"

"I remember," Alexis said, nodding her head, staring at Margaret.

"Your parents decided to send you a few days early so they could have a few days to themselves before driving up from California. It was a last-minute decision." Alexis sat in silence, listening to the story she had lived. "The car explosion that killed your parents was no accident, and it was actually intended to kill you as well."

"I don't understand," Alexis said, her face contorted in disbelief. "Why?"

"We believe Lorcan McCowan was targeting your family to end your bloodline, because of who you are, who you are to become," Margaret explained. "That's why your grandmother had your powers bound and waited to give you the locket until you turned twenty-one. She was hiding you from him until you were ready."

Alexis reached up absently, caressing the locket. "Ready for what?" Alexis asked.

"Ready for the possibility that the vampire would come for you once he discovered you were still alive."

Margaret could tell Alexis was struggling a bit with all the information she had given her. "Take a sip of water, dear," she suggested.

Alexis picked up her glass, downing all its contents. She set the empty glass back down on the table. "I think I'm going to need something a little stronger," she said. "Wine?"

Margaret chuckled a bit. "No, dear, I'm fine."

"Will you excuse me a moment?" Alexis stood, walking towards the kitchen. A few moments later she returned with a glass of white wine. She sat sideways on the sofa, facing this woman who seemed to know more about her family than she did. "What powers?"

"Well, as I mentioned before, you have the ability to heal through touch. You will also have the ability of psychokinesis."

"That's the ability to move things with your mind, right?" Alexis asked.

"That's right," Margaret replied. "I know this is a lot to take in and you have had an exceedingly long day already. Your grandmother had prepared for the possibility of something happening before she could teach you about who you are and your heritage. That is why she wrote the letters to you and left the books on the table downstairs to get you started."

"How is it you know so much about the house and everything in it?" Alexis asked.

Margaret smiled. "I have been here many times. In fact, you and I met many years ago. It was just after your parents died. I was sent by the coven to make sure you and your grandmother were okay."

Alexis paused for a moment before speaking. "You said my parents were killed. Do you believe Gram was also killed?"

"We believe it is a strong possibility," Margaret stated, sorrow in her voice. She and Gram had in fact been remarkably close friends. "I'm sorry to ask you this so soon, but were the circumstances of Charlotte's death unusual to you in any way?"

"Yes," Alexis answered without pause. "They found her in an alley next to a diner, and her keys were locked inside her car parked in front of the building. It looked like she had a stroke or something, and the police figured she was just old or became confused, but Gram was in excellent health."

"Exactly as he would want them to believe," Margaret stated.

"He who, the vampire?"

"Yes," Margaret answered. "The locket you are wearing is to protect you. You probably noticed you feel more connected to your parents and Gram since it was given to you."

"Yes, I do. It also . . ." Alexis paused, almost afraid to say it out loud, but after everything she had learned in the last few hours, anything was possible. "The center of the topaz has . . . *glowed* at me."

Margaret smiled. "It knows who you are. It has begun, my dear."

"What has begun?" Alexis asked.

"It recognizes who you are in the bloodline," Margaret explained. "It knows it belongs to you. It has been blessed to protect you, and as long as you are wearing it, no evil can harm you."

"Does that include vampires?"

"Yes, it does," Margaret said with a smile. "Now, I must be going. Please feel free to call me anytime if you have any questions."

"I will," Alexis said, standing at the same time as Margaret. "Thank you so much for everything. It's just so much to take in."

"I know it is, and for now, just focus on reading through the books that were left out for you on the table," Margaret said. "You have a lot of time to make up for, and if for any reason you cannot reach me, call Claire."

"I will. Thank you again for everything."

Alexis walked Margaret to the door, locking it behind her. She felt even more lost in some ways than she did before. On the other hand, she couldn't believe she was part of some mighty coven. She wondered if Sebastian knew about any of this, or if his parents were keeping him in the dark. Since the females in his family were part of the coven, that meant Sebastian's younger sister, Maxi, was also part of it.

Her head was spinning, and she needed sleep. Tomorrow she would go back down into the basement and start learning about who she was. She turned out all the lights and headed upstairs. She washed her face and changed her clothes. Alexis thought she would have trouble falling asleep with all the new information she had just been given, but she was gone as soon as her head hit the pillow.

CHAPTER 16

Alexis slept surprisingly well despite everything that had happened in the last week. Her thoughts went to Gram and all the changes in her life as she woke the next morning. Change was never easy. Her life was moving in a whole new direction now, and she had so many things to learn. She felt overwhelmed, but she also knew things would eventually get better. She still had the support of Sebastian and his family.

She wasn't that hungry, but she knew she needed to eat. She threw on some sweats and headed downstairs for some coffee and an avocado. She grabbed a knife and spoon and poured her coffee into a travel thermos. She understood now why there was a basket and pulley system right beside the ladder leading down to the basement.

She had not heard from Sebastian, and she appreciated him letting her take the time to work through everything. She would call him later today to fill him in on everything she had discovered. She headed back upstairs to Gram's room. She set her breakfast items down on the dresser next to the window and walked back over to the door of the bedroom. She laughed a bit when she noticed a lock on the door, wondering how she could have missed it for all these years. She closed the door and locked it, walking over to the chest to remove its lock. She opened the top of chest until it was resting against the foot of the bed. She flipped the switch to illuminate the space inside and pulled on the rope to bring the basket up to the top of the ladder, placing her breakfast inside. She climbed down the ladder to the landing, then pulled on the rope to bring the basket down to her. She walked down the stairs to the basement, pausing for a moment at the bottom. She flipped the light on and walked over to the sitting area, setting her breakfast down before walking over to the long table of candles. She lit one of the candles and watched them all come to life, creating a space of warmth and serenity.

Alexis sat down in one of the oversized chairs next to the table, looking around the space for a moment. How many hours had her grandmother spent down here? She still couldn't believe she never knew it existed. How could she have known? It was on another plane of existence, something *else* she never knew about. She removed the top of the thermos and took a sip of her coffee before cutting her avocado in half to eat it. Gazing around the room, she slowly took everything in.

She set her coffee aside and picked up the book on top of the stack in the center of the table. *Psychokinesis for Beginners.* It was a good place to start. She began reading, finding it interesting and a little hard to believe. She wasn't sure about the practical application of it all, but she was sure what she couldn't figure out or learn from the books, Margaret could probably help her with. Alexis already knew how to meditate, and from what she could tell, her new ability was about controlling the mind. She continued reading for quite a while and then decided she would apply what she had learned so far.

Setting the book aside, she stood and walked over towards the candles. She glanced around the room and noticed a large pillow leaning against the chair she had been sitting in. She grabbed it and carried it back to the floor, placing it in front of the table. She sat down on the pillow, crossed her legs, and took a deep breath. She closed her eyes and exhaled, listening to her heartbeat, focusing on her breathing and her internal energy, clearing her mind of everything that had happened in the last week. She focused and practiced calling specific images to mind, holding on to them for a few moments before pushing them away to clear her mind again, just like the book had suggested. As her focus increased, she started to see the images as if they were right in front of her, through closed eyes.

She continued this exercise for quite a while until her tummy started rumbling. She was hungry, and she also felt a little tired. Apparently, honing her skills used a lot of energy. She needed food.

She went back upstairs, and as she walked through the living room to the kitchen, she glanced at the grandfather clock to see it was coming up on two p.m. There was also a message on the machine from Sebastian, calling to see how she was doing. She called him back and asked if he could come over later that night. He was excited to hear from her and offered to bring dinner. Italian. She loved Italian. Alexis made a tuna sandwich and grabbed a glass of water before sitting down at the breakfast table to eat. When she was done, she put her plate and glass in the dishwasher and headed back to the basement. No wonder Gram was in such great shape, running up the stairs all the time!

Alexis reviewed everything she had read so far, deciding to see if she could move the small box of matches on the table. Looking around the room, she knew she was also in need of a clock. Nothing special, just something to help her keep track of time.

She set the box of matches in the center of the large table before sitting down on the pillow. Staring at the box for a few moments, she closed her eyes, focusing on her breathing and on the box, picturing it in her head. She visualized her energy reaching towards the box, encircling it. In her mind, she saw the box rising off the surface of the table. Pushing with her mental energy, she slowly opened her eyes to see the box moving on the table, shifting a bit to the right. Focusing all her energy on the box, she pushed from her solar plexus and her third eye to conjure as much power as she could to move the box. She could feel her energy begin to wane a bit until finally, she lost her focus. The box stopped shifting, and she exhaled loudly.

Frustrated, Alexis decided she just needed a break. Reluctantly, she stood up and stretched a bit before walking over to the table to blow the candles out. She headed back upstairs and locked the chest before leaving Gram's room. It would *always* be Gram's room.

It was a quarter to four, and Sebastian would be over in an hour. She showered quickly and dried off before applying lotion from head to toe. Gram always told her to take care of her skin and to eat right and exercise, because where else was she going to live? Alexis smiled, reflecting on one of her grandmother's favorite sayings. She put on some mascara and a hint of blush, running a brush through her hair and watching as it cascaded around her shoulders. She smiled when she noticed she was starting to look more like her old self, something she was sure Sebastian would be happy to see. She missed him and loved him for understanding she just needed a little time. She tossed on a pair of jeans and a sweater, adding the locket around her neck before putting her shoes on and hurrying downstairs, where she heard the familiar sound of Sebastian's car. She couldn't wait to show him everything.

CHAPTER 17

Alexis threw the door open, rushing forward to plant a kiss on Sebastian's lips, startling him a little at first. She pulled back and stared into his eyes, smiling for the first time in days.

"Hey there," he said, hesitation in his tone.

"Hey there, yourself." She stepped back, noticing the bags of food in his hands. "Let me take one of those for you."

"Thanks," he replied. "Are you okay?"

"Yes, I am," she said, smiling at him. "Come in." She stepped back so he could enter. She closed the door, glancing at him as she moved in the direction of the kitchen. A perplexed look crossed his face, and she couldn't help but laugh.

She walked over to the oven and turned it on warm. She set the bag of food down on the counter, pulling the aluminum containers out to put them in the oven as Sebastian just watched her.

"What are you doing?" he asked, setting the rest of the bags on the countertop.

"We need to keep these warm for a while," she stated with a wink. "There is something I need to show you."

He stared at her for a moment before speaking. "Alexis, are you sure you're okay?"

Laughing again, she understood his concern. She was so different from the last time he'd seen her. "I'm good. I'm just excited to show you something, and you might not believe it . . . at first."

"Okay," he replied. "That sounds ominous."

"It is," she said, taking a few steps closer to him. She reached forward with both hands, placing them on either side of his face.

He smiled, wondering what was going on as she pulled his face towards hers, brushing her lips against his. The kiss was both tender and passionate.

"Well, I'm not sure what you want to show me, but so far I'm intrigued," he said.

"Come with me, please." She laughed, grabbing his hand as she turned to walk out of the kitchen. She led the way through the house, up the stairs to Gram's room. She sensed some reluctance from him as they entered the room, but he followed her over to the chaise lounge. She maneuvered him to sit so he would be facing the chest and she sat down next to him.

"What's going on? Why are we in here?"

"I have to show you something," she replied, smiling. "I have to show you who I really am."

"What do you mean *who you really are*?"

It was going to be a lot for him to take in, and she wanted to do it right. "Remember when I went to go see Mr. Blake, the lawyer, a few days ago?"

"Yes."

"Well, there was a lot of paperwork to sign, specifically for bank accounts, the house, and property, investments, things like that." She paused, studying his face. "I was left with an inheritance to help me finish school, or for whatever I need, as well as an additional inheritance once I turn twenty-five."

"That was great Gram did that for you."

"Yes, it was," she agreed, pausing a moment. "After the funeral, when you dropped me off, I decided to come up here to Gram's room."

Sebastian listened intently, knowing she was going somewhere with her story. He sat in silence, holding her hand as she continued.

"I was standing across the room looking out the window, and as I walked past her bed, I realized I'd never seen inside this chest," she said, gesturing. She walked towards the bed and chest, glancing over her shoulder at Sebastian, a huge grin on her face. He was intrigued. "Gram had always said there were just various things inside the chest, but it was always locked whenever I tried to open it, until a few days ago."

He stood and walked over to join her. "So, what's inside?"

Her smile broadened as Alexis reached down and pulled on the lock, letting it drop to the floor. He watched her open the chest, staring into the darkness, his eyes searching for . . . something. Alexis quietly walked around behind him, reaching inside to flip the light on.

"What the . . ." he asked, taking a step back. "A basement?"

Alexis nodded, grinning from ear to ear. "Come on," she said, climbing down the ladder with Sebastian following her down.

"Alexis, what is this place?"

She reached for the light switch behind the small table, turning the lights on. Sebastian's eyes were filled with wonder and disbelief as she watched him move slowly around the room, taking everything in. The wall of wine, the bookshelves full of books, and the table of candles. He stopped when he noticed the tapestries hanging on the far wall, specifically the one with his family name and crest on it.

"How did we not know about this?" he asked.

"It's a long story I will share with you while we eat," she replied. "There's a lot I need to tell you."

Sebastian walked over to the tapestries, reaching out with his right hand, tracing the outline of his family crest with his fingertips.

"My parents have got some explaining to do, that's for sure," he stated, smiling at Alexis. "We are destined to be together." They had never really talked about the future, marriage and family, but he always knew she was the one for him. He knew it in the depths of his soul.

She walked over to him and kissed him passionately before pulling back, gazing into his eyes. "I've missed you so much the last few days."

"I've missed you too," he replied. "I didn't want to crowd you though."

"Thank you for that," she said, smiling. "Now, let's go eat. I'm starving."

Over the next hour, Alexis explained everything she had learned, from Gram's letter and from Margaret. She filled him in on all the reading and studying she was doing as well as Lorcan McCowan, the one responsible for the death of her parents.

"Vampire?" he asked. "Seriously?"

"Yes."

"And he's around four hundred years old?"

"Exactly." Alexis went on to explain how much reading she had done so far and how much more there was to learn. "The whole concept of psychokinesis is incredible. In fact, just before I called you, I think I was about to have a breakthrough."

"Really?" Sebastian asked. "Do you want to show me?"

"Actually, I do," she stated. "First, let's get these dishes in the dishwasher, and then I need to go into Gram's study. I'm looking for any other books she may have that I need to read."

They cleared the dishes and headed into the study. Alexis felt like she was viewing the room in a whole new light. The cozy sitting area and the bookshelves that took up an entire wall were so much more now than just a wall of books. Now, it was a resource for her destiny.

"Is there a specific title or subject matter you're looking for?" he asked.

"Anything to do with mental or healing abilities, I guess," she responded. "Why don't you start at the far end, and I'll start at this end, and we can meet in the middle."

"Sounds like a plan." Sebastian walked to the far end of the bookshelves. In the corner, there was a sculpture he had seen a few times in a picture but never in real life. He wondered if it was the original or a replica. It wouldn't surprise him if it were an original, especially after everything Alexis had told him. He also had a feeling his parents would be able to answer any questions they might have, shed light on things they couldn't find the answers to. His eyes scanned the different titles on the shelves.

"Oh my gosh," she exclaimed. "I don't believe it."

"What is it?" he asked, walking over to her.

"This book," she said, holding up a copy of *Heidi*. "Gram used to read this to me all the time when I was little. It became my favorite bedtime story. In fact, she read it to me so many times I'm surprised the binding is still holding together." Alexis began thumbing through the book, stopping in the middle when she found a piece of paper tucked inside.

"What's that?"

"I don't know," she said, pulling the piece of paper out and handing the book to him. She carefully opened the paper and began reading aloud.

Alexis,

Your past is the foundation for your future. It holds good memories like the book Heidi *and bad memories like the loss of your family. But all these memories help make you who you are, and some may hold a key to your future. Never forget, your family will always be with you.*

Love,
Gram
P.S. Please return the book to the shelf just as you found it.

"That's odd," he said after she finished reading the note.

She chuckled. "It is." Then she paused. "And it's not."

She looked at him, and he could tell something was up.

Alexis knew Gram well enough to know those specific instructions were to be followed. She gestured, and he handed the book back to her. He watched as she put the book back on the shelf, pausing for a moment before she pushed it slowly towards the back of the shelf. One final push and the open edge of the book touched the wall. Alexis and Sebastian both took a step back when they heard a noise behind the wall and then a click. The far end of the bookshelves released, swinging away from them slightly. A hint of light shone from inside the wall. She glanced at him before stepping forward.

"Hey, what are you doing?"

"If I'm right, getting down to the basement just got a lot easier." She pushed the bookshelves away from her and stepped onto the landing behind the wall leading down to the basement. "Come on. I have more to show you."

CHAPTER 18

Proficiency was her goal. Over the next few weeks, Alexis spent even more time in the basement reading and practicing her new abilities. She was getting stronger, and in addition to making the small box of matches float, she could call a specific book from the shelf in the study. They didn't always make it across the entire room to her, but she knew very soon they would. She also noticed she felt more connected to her abilities when she was wearing the locket, like somehow it gave her a boost of power while she was wearing it. So she wore it often while she was practicing but noticed she still maintained her abilities without it.

Sebastian helped her with research and ran drills with her, specifically techniques to increase her mental strength and control, borrowing on the principles he learned in the military and martial arts. There would be times maintaining a cool head and staying calm would be an asset. She also spent more time training with Josh, working on her ground game and sparring. Now that she knew there was a specific threat out there targeting her, she wanted as much knowledge and skill as possible. She had no idea if Lorcan McCowan was still a threat, but she decided she would rather be safe than sorry.

Alexis loved sparring with Sebastian in the ring, but it always ended with a kiss. He would pin her, then lean in.

"That's cheating," she would say, trying to suppress her laughter.

"All is fair in love and war, baby," he would reply.

She caught him off guard one day, using her hips to throw him off balance, and she pinned *him* instead. She laughed when she did it, and the look of surprise on his face was priceless.

"BEST STUDENT EVER!" Josh called from outside the ring. "That was some great ingenuity you used for that move, Alexis."

"Thanks, Teach!" she responded with enthusiasm. She was thankful to have both men in her life. She knew they cared about her, and that helped give her strength.

Alexis managed to stay busy with all her activities, yet there *were* still moments when the loss of Gram could make her cry. They were seldom, but if Sebastian was there when it happened, he would wrap his arms around her, making everything better.

She still had not heard anything from Nika. At first, she was concerned. Now she felt disappointed and angry. They had always been so close, ever since their sophomore year of high school.

They originally met when Alexis and her family were still living in California. They didn't know each other very well back then and never spent any time together outside of school. It wasn't until Nika and her family moved up from California, after Alexis lost her parents, that she and Nika became fast friends. Nika came from a wealthy background and always had the best of everything. Alexis was happy with the things Gram provided, but her grandmother was always rather modest with her spending.

Despite the differences between them, Alexis and Nika became inseparable. Nika had always been rather generous with her, taking her shopping or treating her to a night out, never asking for anything in return. Alexis accepted Nika for who she was and not because of her wealth, which Nika had thanked her for a few times throughout their friendship. It was one of the reasons she always defended Nika to Sebastian. Sure, they were different, but there had always been a bond between them. Now, Alexis had no idea what they had or if there was a friendship to speak of. She had no idea if Nika was all right or even if she was back in town. All she knew was she missed her friend, despite her disappointment.

Sebastian's family invited her over to spend Thanksgiving with them, and she was excited to see everybody, especially Claire, Sebastian's mother. There were a few questions Margaret couldn't seem to answer over the phone. Having somebody in the same state was going to be better. Claire was already working with Maxi, Sebastian's younger sister, who had just turned seventeen. Maxi had received her powers when she was sixteen, and Alexis was excited to learn what abilities she had, compared to her own. Everything seemed so hush-hush.

"It's something the coven strictly enforces," Claire explained to her on the phone one night. "They want those who are going to have the power to be introduced to it slowly, and it was also especially important the outside world never find out about them. Waiting until a young lady turned sixteen, as well as hiding it from anyone else in the family who didn't need to know initially, was the best way to keep the secret."

"So how did Sebastian take the news?" Alexis asked.

"Honestly, he was not as surprised as we thought he would be," Claire stated. "His father and I had a feeling he knew things were different in our home."

"Why am I not surprised to hear that?" Alexis said, laughing.

"You've got a good one there, my dear," Claire said. "And I'm not just saying that because he is my son."

"I know how lucky I am," she replied. "I am *so* grateful to have all of you in my life, especially after losing Gram."

"Charlotte was a lovely person," Claire said. "You actually remind me of her a bit. You also remind me of your mother. I know you draw strength from both."

"Thank you, Claire," she said.

"You're welcome. We look forward to seeing you tomorrow for Thanksgiving. So make sure you bring your appetite."

She laughed. "That will not be a problem. Between all the different types of training I've been doing, I'm eating like a horse these days."

Claire laughed. "That's one upside. We seem to burn lots of calories, and it's my understanding healers burn even more calories than others."

"As long as I don't start eating more than Sebastian, I think I'll be okay," she said with a chuckle.

They said their good-byes, and for the first time in weeks, she felt like she had a sense of family again in her life. She didn't feel alone anymore, and she doubted she ever would again.

CHAPTER 19

The phone was ringing, and Alexis figured it was Sebastian reminding her about the pies, one chocolate and one pumpkin. She had found Gram's recipes a few days ago and decided to try her hand at making them. Hopefully, they were good. She grabbed the phone by the fourth ring, surprised by the voice on the other end. "Hello?"

"Hi, Alexis."

"Nika!" she exclaimed. "How are you? Where are you?"

"I'm great," Nika replied. "I just got back into town a few weeks ago and had to take care of some things."

Alexis sat down on her bed. "I left you a few messages, but I never heard back from you. I was getting a little worried."

"Yeah, sorry about that," she replied, sounding blasé. "I've just been *so* busy lately."

Alexis couldn't believe this was her best friend. She sounded detached and completely disinterested. "I really missed you." She paused a moment. "I lost Gram." Silence was all she heard from the other end of the phone. "Nika?"

"Yeah, I'm here," Nika replied. "Sorry about that. Hey, I've gotta go, but we'll catch up soon, 'kay?"

The line dropped before Alexis could reply. She stared at the handset for a moment before hanging up. That was weird and rude. Nika could be rude, off in her own world from time to time, but she had never been that dismissive towards Alexis. Maybe something had happened in Paris. Maybe Nika and her family were dealing with a family matter, something she could certainly relate to. She stood up and walked back into the bathroom to finish getting ready for the day. She figured her friend would tell her what was going on when the time was right.

CHAPTER 20

It was the first holiday without Gram, yet Alexis was grateful to be celebrating Thanksgiving with Sebastian and his family, thankful they were now part of her family. The tapestries in the basement declared it.

She heard a knock on the door as she was putting the pies into a travel container. Walking to the door, she decided not to mention the strange phone call she had gotten from Nika earlier, especially since Sebastian wasn't Nika's biggest fan. Today was about celebration and happiness. Whatever was going on with Nika would have to wait.

"Hey there, pretty girl," he said when she opened the door.

"Hey there, yourself," she replied, leaning forward to kiss him. "I'm ready, I just need to put my coat on."

Sebastian stepped towards the closet to retrieve her coat, helping her put it on. She loved how chivalrous he was. While she adjusted the buttons and collar, he picked up the pies from the table near the door.

"You ready?" he asked.

"I am," she replied, glancing around the living room for a moment.

"Are you okay?" he asked, gently squeezing her shoulder.

"Yes, it's crazy to think how different things were just a month ago."

"I know you miss her, Alexis," he said. "I do too."

"I know you do," she replied with a smile.

"You can do this," he said.

"I know, because you will always be there for me," she replied softly.

He pulled her in for a hug, kissing her softly on her neck. She pulled back, looking into his eyes. "There is no other place I would rather be."

"Thank you."

"Always," he replied, kissing her gently on the lips. "Now, let's go eat some turkey," he said, reaching for the door. "Mom said you were hungry these days."

She laughed and followed him out of the house. Stepping out into the crisp November afternoon, she realized she really was going to be okay.

They arrived at his parents' house ten minutes later, and she couldn't believe how beautifully the house was decorated for the season. Sebastian helped her with her coat, hanging it on the rack in the entryway. He headed off to the kitchen to deliver the pies, and she walked into the living room to join the festivities.

"Alexis, my dear," Claire said, approaching her with open arms. "You look gorgeous."

Alexis had worn a long-sleeved garnet-colored blouse with a tea-length, black A-line skirt and tall black leather boots. Her hair was swept up off her neck in a messy ponytail, her makeup a little more dramatic than usual. She welcomed Claire's embrace. "Thank you. Everything looks beautiful," she replied.

"The locket looks great on you," Claire stated.

Alexis touched it with her right hand. "It's crazy because it actually seems to know me."

Claire laughed. "That's because of who you are. It knows you are part of the bloodline and the coven. Always remember, it can increase your power, as well as protect you against evil."

"Good to know," she replied.

"Would you like a glass of wine?" Claire asked.

"Yes, please."

Alexis was watching Claire walk over to the bar on the far side of the living room when she saw Maxi. It had been a while since she had seen the girl, and she couldn't believe how grown up she looked, especially since she was only seventeen.

"Alexis," Maxi called, walking over to give her a hug.

"What have you been up to these days?" Alexis asked.

"Well, same as you," she said with a wink.

She couldn't help but laugh. "But you got a head start on me."

"True. I have been working on my skills for the past year," Maxi stated before she lowered her voice. "I'm sorry I didn't really get a chance to speak with you at the gathering for your grandmother."

"It's okay," Alexis replied. "I wasn't really up for conversation that day."

"I'm so glad you're here," Maxi said, giving her another hug.

She hugged her back, their bond feeling stronger than ever. "Me too."

"Hey, there's two of my favorite girls," Sebastian said, slipping in between them, his arms draped over their shoulders.

"*Two* of your favorite girls?" Alexis asked. "How many do you have, mister?"

He just winked at her, and Maxi punched him in the arm as she broke free to help her mother with the drinks.

"She thinks she's so tough," Sebastian said, watching his younger sister. Alexis could tell he was proud.

"She has you for an older brother. She'd better be."

Just as Claire brought Alexis her wine, the doorbell chimed.

"Be right back," Sebastian said.

Claire and Alexis walked across the room to sit down on the sofa when Sebastian and Josh walked into the room. Alexis couldn't help but smile when she saw the two men together. They were both dressed in slacks and button-down shirts. Just looking at them, nobody could ever imagine how dangerous they really were. Thankfully, they were the good guys. They walked over to join everybody sitting in the living room.

"It looks like the two of you could use something to drink," Claire said.

"I've got it, Mom," Maxi said suddenly. "A beer, right, Josh?" she asked, beaming at him.

"That would be great," he replied. "Thanks, kiddo."

Alexis watched the smile fade as Maxi turned to get the beer for Josh. Alexis smiled and winked at him. "What?" he asked.

"I think somebody likes you," she whispered, nodding in Maxi's direction.

"Funny," he replied. "She's a bit young for me, don't you think?" He sat down in a chair across from her.

"And let's not forget my *baby* sister," Sebastian said. "I'd hate to have to kick your ass."

Josh chuckled. "You mean *try*."

They all laughed as Maxi returned with a beer for Josh and her brother.

"So, where's Dennis?" Alexis asked, referring to Sebastian's father.

"Oh, he's in the kitchen making sure the turkey is going to be perfect," Claire announced with pride. "In fact, I should go check on the two of them."

She stood, heading towards the kitchen, and Maxi took her spot on the sofa beside Alexis.

"So tell me, what can you do?" Maxi asked.

"Not too much just yet," she began. "I've been working on psychokinesis, you know, trying to move objects with my mind. So far, I've been able to float a small box of matches and move a few books. Of course, I've only been working on developing my skills for a few weeks now. There's been a lot of reading, and I haven't even attempted my healing powers yet."

"Moving stuff with your mind would be awesome," Maxi announced with envy. "I'm learning how to be a tracker. How boring is that?"

"Now, Maxi," Claire said, entering the room with Dennis. "Your abilities are just as important as anybody else's."

"Not to mention, the fact that your brother is teaching you how to fight and protect innocents," Sebastian stated.

"That's true, I guess," she agreed, her spirits lifted. Alexis could see how much she idolized her brother. "So when are you going to test your healing abilities?"

"How about now," Dennis said, stepping forward. "It seems one of the racks in the oven and I had a slight disagreement." He held up his left arm, showing everybody a swollen red mark on the underside of his wrist.

Maxi stood up so her father could sit down next to Alexis.

"I'm not sure how to do this," she stated.

"Just remember the principles you apply with the psychokinesis," Sebastian said. "Focus on what you want to do, what you want to happen. Focus on the result."

Alexis looked around the room. All eyes were on her. She laughed nervously. "Okay," she said. "Here we go."

She sat forward on the sofa, taking Dennis's hand in her left hand. She allowed her right hand, the power hand, to hover about an inch over the wound. Heat from it instantly heated up her own hand. She closed her eyes, taking deep breaths, calling for the inflammation from the burn to come to her. She could feel the heat from his arm rising to meet her hand before she asked it to dissipate into the air. Then she changed her focus, this time asking for the area to be cooled, pushing her energy back down into his wrist from the palm of her hand, asking the pain to leave the area and picturing his skin healthy again. She heard whispers and a soft gasp. Dennis squeezed her hand. She opened her eyes to see his arm was healed. She couldn't believe she had done it.

"Thank you," he said, beaming at her.

"You're welcome. Wow." Alexis closed her eyes, sitting back into the sofa.

"Are you okay?" Sebastian asked.

She shook her head a little, opening her eyes slowly to look at him. "I'm okay, just a little dizzy, and hungry now." The room erupted in laughter.

"That is part of the gift, my dear," Claire said. "You are using more energy. That's why you've been so hungry lately."

"That makes sense."

"You wouldn't believe how much I started eating in the last year," Maxi said, laughing.

"Well then, I think it's time to go into the dining room," Dennis announced. He stood up, offering his hand to Alexis.

The rest of the afternoon was full of love and laughter, as well as delicious food. After their meal, everybody gathered back in the living room for coffee and dessert. They talked about some of the things happening in the world, as well as Christmas being just around the corner.

Around eight p.m., Alexis asked Sebastian to take her home.

"Is everything okay?" he asked quietly.

"Yes," she replied. "I've missed you," she said with a wink.

He smiled, understanding perfectly. She thanked his parents for the wonderful meal and hospitality as they made their way to the door. Josh headed out at the same time, thanking Sebastian's parents, as always, for making him feel like part of the family.

Alexis and Sebastian spent the rest of the evening making up for the last few weeks, before falling asleep in each other's arms.

CHAPTER 21

A break was needed, and fun was to be had. Since Sebastian was away for his Reserves weekend, Alexis called Maxi to see if she wanted to join her for Christmas shopping. Maxi was thrilled and jumped at the chance.

It was the beginning of December, and sales were in full swing. They arrived at the mall, starting their search at JCPenney laughing and talking about clothes and boys. In many ways, Maxi reminded Alexis of herself when she was seventeen years old, excited about new outfits and school dances, wondering which boy was going to ask her out. Walking through the mall, they stopped in a few of the smaller shops on their way to Frederick & Nelson to have lunch in the Frango Restaurant. Once seated, Alexis reflected on a few times Gram had brought her here to eat. Maxi didn't miss a beat.

"You miss her a lot," Maxi stated in a soft voice, concerned she might be getting too personal.

Alexis looked up at her and smiled. "I do. I knew the holidays were going to be tough but . . . Do you want to eat someplace else?" she asked, looking around the restaurant.

"No." Maxi reminded her so much of Sebastian sometimes, certain gestures and how in tune she was to the emotions of others. "The food is great here."

"Okay."

Maxi picked up her menu, reading through all the amazing choices listed. She had only been to the restaurant a few times, but she always enjoyed herself, especially when they had the seasonal fashion shows, offering a look at the upcoming fashions while you enjoyed your meal.

The waitress came by and took their order, and soon their food was on the table.

"Have you thought about what you're going to do after high school?" Alexis asked.

"My mom wants me to go to Oregon, where the coven is, so I can study and learn from the old masters." Maxi poked at her food randomly.

"What do *you* want to do?"

She smiled. "I would love to do some traveling, backpacking through Europe or something. I want to see the world."

"Well, maybe someday you and I can go on a trip together," Alexis said.

"Really?" she asked with enthusiasm. "Just the two of us?"

"Absolutely," Alexis replied. "We'll go check out the world."

Maxi beamed with excitement. She was really enjoying herself. Alexis didn't treat her like a child, she spoke to her like she was an adult.

"Can I ask you something?" Maxi asked.

"Sure," she replied. She studied the young girl's face, realizing Maxi had just become rather serious in contrast to the previous carefree conversation.

"Well, it's about a guy I sorta like, except I think he likes somebody else, somebody he probably shouldn't like, and I just wish he would like me like I like him." Maxi paused long enough to inhale deeply before exhaling loudly.

Alexis stifled a laugh, smiling instead. Maxi was confiding in her, and she didn't want her to feel like her feelings were being belittled. "Are you talking about Josh?"

Maxi's eyes widened, her hands covering her now open mouth. "Yes! Oh my gosh! He is so beautiful! Wait, can a man be beautiful? Is that weird? Oh wow! I can't believe I finally said it out loud." She erupted in laughter, and Alexis joined in.

"Yes, a man can be beautiful," Alexis declared, "but, Maxi, he is a little too old for you, don't you think? Not to mention, I think your brother would have a serious problem with it."

"I know," she replied. "He is just so . . ."

Alexis could feel Maxi's frustration across the table. Maxi stared at her for a moment before dropping her eyes, poking at the rest of her food with her fork. Alexis wasn't sure what to say.

"I know it's frustrating to like somebody when they don't seem to share your same feelings, but surely there is a boy or two at school who you find interesting."

"But that's just it, they're *boys*," Maxi stated. "Josh is certainly not a boy."

"No, he isn't, and if you were older, the difference in your ages wouldn't matter," Alexis explained.

"It still wouldn't work," Maxi announced, a smile creeping across her face.

"What do you mean?"

"It wouldn't matter because of you, Alexis."

She was confused. She certainly didn't have a problem with Maxi liking Josh. Maxi started laughing, leaving her even more confused. "What are you talking about?" she asked.

"I'm talking about the fact that Josh likes you."

Alexis sat back in her seat, staring at Maxi, watching her nod. She didn't know what to say.

"It's true, I've felt it," Maxi declared.

"Okay, now I'm really confused," Alexis confessed. "What do you mean, you felt it?"

"It's part of my tracker abilities," Maxi explained, her face taking on a more serious look. "I can sense a person's intentions." She paused for a moment, studying Alexis's face. "The longer a person is in one place, the more I can learn about their intentions. It's like their energy burns an impression in that location, which then helps me determine where they will go next."

"You mean like an empath?"

"No, that's you, which ties into your healing abilities," Maxi clarified. "Don't worry though. Josh has no intention of ever acting on what he feels towards you. He cares about my brother and their friendship way too much, and believe me, I would never tell my brother because I know no good would ever come of it."

"I had no idea," Alexis began. "Wait, why are you telling me this?"

"Because you've started training now, and you were bound to pick up on his emotions sooner or later," she replied. "I didn't want you to be caught off guard."

"I appreciate the heads-up, although I'm not sure what to do with this information."

"Just keep it to yourself," she stated plainly. "No need to tell anybody. It's our little secret." Maxi reached across the table, offering Alexis her pinky finger, the childlike expression having returned to her face. Laughing, they made a pinky swear of silence on the matter.

They finished their lunch, and Alexis paid the bill, her head still spinning from the information Maxi had shared. Alexis didn't like keeping secrets from Sebastian, but Maxi was right; no good could ever come of Josh's feelings being revealed, and since he had always shown nothing but respect, there really was no reason to tell anybody. Now that she thought about it, despite his "cool" demeanor, there *were* times when Josh seemed to spend a second longer than he needed looking at her. She just figured it was who he was or perhaps part of his military training.

They walked back down to the other end of the mall towards the car, laughing and talking about the progress they had made buying Christmas presents so far, but they knew there would be another day of shopping soon.

After she dropped Maxi off, Alexis headed over to Aidan's gallery. She had not been there since her grandmother had died. She missed the art world, and now that she was no longer in school, she didn't spend a lot of time looking at art. Maybe when she got home, she would flip through some of her favorite coffee-table books.

She parked across from the gallery just as the sun was setting, then dashed across the street to enter the building. It would be closing in about a half hour, which didn't give her much time to look around. Still, she felt a sense of calm come over her when she walked through the doors. It was *her* world. She headed over to the Impressionist section, taking a moment to linger in front of one of her favorites.

"So nice to see you again, Miss Alexis," a familiar voice said.

She jumped a bit, turning around quickly. "Aidan, hello."

"My apologies, I didn't mean to startle you. I haven't seen you for some time. I hope everything is well with you."

"Actually . . ." Her gaze dropped for a moment as she found her voice. "I lost my grandmother recently, so I've been busy taking care of . . . *things*."

He stepped forward, taking one of her hands in his. "I'm sorry to hear about your loss," he said. "Was it sudden?"

"Yes, it was," she replied. His touch was strangely comforting. There was just something about him. She pulled her hand away, turning slightly, her attention back on the art piece in front of her. "I've had to make a few adjustments recently, like withdrawing from my classes, and I miss the artwork I used to see daily. I guess you could say I came in here to get my . . . fix."

"You are always welcome here," he said, smiling. "So, where is your boyfriend this evening?"

"He's away for the weekend on business."

"His business must be important to take him away from you for an entire weekend," he stated.

Alexis didn't know why she suddenly wanted to keep her life with Sebastian private. "He'll be back Sunday night. Well, I should probably get going so you can close."

Aidan smiled. "It was nice seeing you again, and do come back soon."

"Thank you," she replied. "Have a nice evening."

Leaving the gallery, she walked quickly to her car. On the short drive home, her mind went back to the conversation with Aidan. He seemed different than when she first met him. Maybe it was just her whole new outlook on life. She smiled as she pulled into the driveway and turned the engine off. Once inside, she went upstairs to change, getting comfortable. She ordered a pizza and decided it was movie night. She checked the kitchen for some wine to go with the pizza. The open bottle only had half a glass remaining in it, so she headed down to the basement to retrieve another bottle.

After the pizza arrived, she took a few pieces and a glass of wine into the den to watch her movie. It was one of her favorite kinds of evenings. Relaxing and quiet.

CHAPTER 22

The rest of the holiday season was filled with laughter and love as Alexis spent Christmas Eve and Christmas Day with Sebastian and his family. Josh was invited, too, so he wouldn't be alone. Nobody really knew if Josh had any remaining family, and Sebastian didn't ask. It was part of the guy code.

For New Year's Eve, Sebastian and Alexis escaped for a week, staying at a romantic cabin resort, courtesy of his parents. Their room was equipped with a huge shower for two and a hot tub on the deck to soak their sore muscles after a day of hiking. Sitting in the hot tub together, they would gaze up at the stars, the cold night air on their faces. Basking in the warmth of the cabin and Sebastian's arms every night was quite the contrast to the mountains, blanketed in heavy snow outside. Alexis was in heaven.

She continued to find opportunities to practice her skills, whether it be psychokinesis or healing, especially when Sebastian injured himself during a hike. A twisted ankle proved to be somewhat problematic until they returned to their room, and she laid hands on him. Within moments, the swelling and bruising disappeared.

"You are becoming handier than a Swiss Army knife," he said, smiling at her.

"A lady does what she can." She closed her eyes, and a bottle of wine floated over the top of the bar area to the table where they were sitting. She reached for it, setting it down on the table between them. "Wine?"

He laughed, standing up to retrieve the wine stems from the kitchen. "Thanks again for fixing my ankle," he said, sitting back down with the glasses and the bottle opener.

"It was my pleasure, sir," she said, leaning forward to drop a passionate kiss on his lips.

The remaining days in the cabin passed quickly, and soon they were bringing in the New Year. Alexis couldn't imagine a better way to celebrate.

CHAPTER 23

Being back in Seattle was strange for Nika. It never really felt like home, mostly because she was originally from California. When she first moved to Washington State with her parents, she thought the rain would drive her insane. Now, Seattle suited her. California *would* be a difficult place to avoid the sun.

Once she was settled, *He* called to let her know there was an assignment for her. An associate, the manager at his nightclub, was conducting the sort of business that could attract the wrong kind of attention, attention from the authorities. It was rumored Mr. Rico was selling drugs as a side business out of the club, and *He* didn't want the authorities looking his way. Nika was to go to the club and persuade Mr. Rico it would be in his best interest to either stop his little side business or leave town. Nika was excited about the assignment. It was nice to be needed, and it made her feel important. Besides, she always enjoyed clubbing.

She entered the club, asking to speak with the manager. The staff was used to pretty girls asking for Mr. Rico, so to them she looked like just another pretty face who wanted to spend time with him. Apparently, he was quite the ladies' man.

She wandered further into the club, getting a look at the dance floor, enjoying all the bodies as they moved to the pulsating beat of the music. So many options to choose from, but that wasn't why she was there. She needed to stay focused. Several men stared at her, and she smiled. *Who could blame them?* She knew she looked gorgeous in her short, fitted, dark red dress, her hair swept up in a French twist, a few wispy strands framing her face.

A petite young lady appeared in front of her wearing a short black dress, looking more like a uniform than a fashion statement, her long blonde hair pulled back in a high ponytail and her face adorned with pink and lavender shades on her eyes and lips. She looked like one of the many blonde girls Nika used to see all the time when she lived in California, except this girl was clearly not from California, just a knock-off. She was a little taller than Nika but not by much.

"My name is Mia," the girl spouted with a bit of attitude. Nika smiled smugly at the silly little twit. "Mr. Rico will see you now. Please follow me."

Mia turned, walking quickly ahead of her, attempting to make Nika chase after her. It didn't work. Nika moved at her own pace, a serene smile across her face. She followed the girl down the hallway towards a staircase she had passed earlier when she was watching the dancers.

Mia stopped midway up the stairs to wait for Nika to catch up, annoyed at the woman's arrogant attitude. She knew immediately she didn't like the redhead. Mia continued walking up the rest of the stairs, looking behind her one last time before proceeding down the long hallway to the last door on the right, where she waited for Nika to join her.

"Mr. Rico is waiting for you." Mia knocked once before opening the door.

"Of course, he is a sweetie," Nika purred, walking past the girl. "And I ask that we *not* be disturbed." Before the girl could reply, Nika slammed the door in her face.

Mia stood outside the door for a moment before walking away. She laughed to herself, moving quickly down the hall to return to the main level. She knew the redhead wouldn't be around long. Mr. Rico preferred his women to be a lot more submissive.

Nika glanced around the room, noticing all the women who surrounded the handsome Hispanic man sitting on the love seat. Apparently, he took this piece of furniture to heart. She smiled. "Mr. Rico?"

His chocolate-brown eyes drank in every inch of her face and body, and she immediately wanted to kill him. *Such nerve.*

"I am Mr. Rico," he announced, sitting back casually on the love seat. The women on either side of him glanced at him, smirking when they looked back at Nika. Everybody in the room looked like they were ready to appear in a fashion show. She had to give them credit, they really knew how to dress, but their attitudes were almost more than she could stand.

She smiled back sweetly, knowing no matter what, she was the one in charge. "The boss sent me."

"As a gift, I imagine," Rico stated, licking his lips, his gaze lingering on her hips for a moment before traveling down her legs. "The boss is most generous with his offering."

That was it. *How in the world could this little man be so presumptuous?* Her smile didn't waver. "If it pleases you, I would like to have a word, in private."

"Mm, now *that* I will agree to," he announced, his wicked smile broadening. "Ladies, would you leave us, please?"

She watched the line of women walk towards the door. There had to be at least a dozen of them throughout the room. The two sitting with him each kissed him on the lips before exiting the office. He stood, walking towards her in what she suspected was his best jungle cat prowess. He wore a custom-made black suit with a bright colored blue dress shirt underneath, which would probably normally enhance his appeal, until he either opened his mouth or looked directly at you. Not even the finest of clothes could make up for his sleazy demeanor. She stood still as he circled her, leaning in to sniff her as he moved around behind her. He was wearing expensive cologne and obviously believed himself to be incredibly smooth. *Some men are just full of delusions.*

She was really going to enjoy this.

"Mm, you are a *beautiful* woman," he said, staring into her eyes. "Won't you join me?" He offered his hand. She took it, following him over to the love seat. Once they sat, Mr. Rico slid his left arm across the back, leaning in closer to her, his hot breath in her face. "Now, where shall we begin?"

"Mr. Rico," she began softly, batting her eyes. "The boss has been hearing some things regarding his club and your activities, and I hate to tell you this, but he's not happy."

"Is that so?" He sat back from her slightly. "I'm guessing he sent you down here to ask me to stop whatever it is he *thinks* I'm doing?"

"Yes, that's right," she replied. "Either stop what you are doing or leave town. Those are your options."

Rico laughed out loud, drowning out the salsa music softly playing in the background. "Well, I have a third option."

"And what might that be?"

He leaned even closer, and Nika held her ground. Boldly, he reached down in her lap, picking up her left hand. "How about you tell Mr. Boss Man I accept his generous gift." He nodded towards her as he brought her hand up to his lips, kissing it. "And I will continue to do what I'm doing, as he remains the silent owner."

She couldn't help but smile at the fool in front of her. She could smell his excitement, and his arrogance filled the room. "I'll tell you what," she began. "I have a counteroffer for you instead." She leaned in closer to him.

"Mm, I think I'm going to like this," he said.

She leaned all the way over so her mouth was right beside his ear, the stench of his cologne almost more than she could stand. "I accept your resignation, Mr. Rico," she whispered.

Mr. Rico started to laugh, pulling back to look at her. His smile faded when he noticed her fangs, and before he could move, Nika grabbed the back of his head with her right hand. She leaned forward, sinking her teeth into the left side of his neck, draining him dry before snapping his neck. She watched as the lifeless body hit the floor, making a loud thud. She stood, smoothing her dress before walking over to the wet bar to pour herself a glass of champagne. The office door opened, and some of Mr. Rico's ladies entered the room, gasping when they saw him lying on the floor. She took a sip of champagne before looking at them.

"Your services are no longer required," Nika said with a smile. "You should leave."

CHAPTER 24

Security would be along shortly, because she knew there was no way all those women suddenly leaving didn't attract attention.

Nika downed the rest of the champagne, refilling her glass before scanning the room, taking in the décor. She knew exactly what she wanted now, and she was sure *He* would be okay with it. She was going to be the new manager, the new face of the nightclub. She would bring style and elegance to what was once a mediocre establishment. At least Mr. Rico had good taste in champagne.

She moved around the room, noting the potential of the space. Oversized windows filled the outside wall, giving her the opportunity to dress them up with some lavish color. She needed to look around the rest of the club to better assess what else needed to be done. Probably not an entire facelift, but a good sprucing up. No need having the club out of commission and not bringing in money for an extended period. Just a few special touches here and there.

She walked back over to the love seat and sat down, pleased with her ideas so far for the remodel, when two men from security rushed into the room. She casually looked over at them, watching their eyes become enlarged when they saw the body on the floor, just to the left of her feet. One of the men looked to be in great shape, taller with a wonderfully developed physique, while the other just looked like a meathead. He was shorter, mostly bald but at one time looked to have had red hair. To make up for his bald head, he sported a mustache and a tiny red beard. His beady blue eyes were filled with confusion and anger when he saw Mr. Rico on the floor.

"Hello, boys," she said with a smile. They looked at each other, then back at her. "I'm going to need you to take this trash out for me," she stated without looking down. Nika took another sip of champagne, waiting for their questions. Her calm demeanor confused them, and she felt stimulated by the mystery and allure they felt. She had no idea what kind of rapport they'd had with Mr. Rico, and quite frankly, it no longer mattered.

"Who is this chick?" the bigger one asked the other man. "Just who the hell are you?" He took a step closer to her.

"Oh good," she said, leaning forward to set her glass down on the coffee table. She stood slowly and walked over to them. "You do understand what I'm saying."

"And *I* asked who the hell you were?" the bigger one demanded, taking another step closer.

Nika looked deep into his eyes, smiling sweetly. "I am the one in charge here, understand?"

"Sorry, sweetheart, but I don't take orders from women," the big man announced, closing the distance between them, attempting to completely intimidate her.

"You sure about that?" She held her position and his gaze, allowing her eyes to flare, flashing bright green just for a moment before returning to their normal color. The larger man took a few steps back. "That's better. What are your names?"

"Mick, but everybody calls me Big Mick, and this is Adam," the larger man answered.

Adam wasn't sure who she was or what she had done to Mick, but he would do whatever she asked. He never heard anybody speak to Big Mick that way, especially a woman. Well, maybe just the one time.

"The boss sent me here to ask Mr. Rico to stop whatever illegal business he had going on, and well, Mr. Rico was not happy with that request. Needless to say"—she cast a glance behind her, smirking—"we came to another arrangement." The men looked at each other and back at her, both listening carefully. "I'm sure the police have already been called by at least a few of the women who rushed out of here, so I need you to act quickly and dispose of this mess," she said, walking back to the love seat. She took a seat, retrieving her glass of champagne at the same time. "Now please, do as I've asked, and we won't have any more undue fuss."

Big Mick looked at Adam, gesturing for him to close the door as he walked over to a large throw draped across the back of an oversized chair. He picked it up and went back around to the body, hesitant to get too close to the woman. He had no idea who or what she was, but he knew she was deadly. Big Mick worked quickly, tucking the fabric around the body, adjusting it until the entire body was covered. He stood, picking the body up in one motion and throwing it over his shoulder like a sack of potatoes.

Nika studied the two men, pleased they were both larger than the average man. It was nice to know she would have some muscle around in case she needed it.

She continued watching the well-built man, his eyes never leaving her. "Adam?" she began. "Is there a way to get rid of the body without having others see it?"

"There is actually an incinerator downstairs in the basement," he stated, his voice calmer than she expected. "We will take care of it for you, Miss . . ."

"Nika," she replied with a smile. "Thank you, Adam." She liked him already.

Big Mick gestured for Adam to open the door, and he moved quickly through the opening and across the hall. He was happy to put some distance between himself and the woman. Adam smiled again, bowing slightly as he began shutting the door.

"Adam," she called after him. "Please escort the police officers in for me. They are just parking their car."

Not wanting to know how she knew they had arrived, he simply nodded and closed the door. He walked quickly down the hall, and just as he stepped off the last step to the main floor, Mia directed the police officers to where he was standing.

"Good evening, officers," Adam said calmly. "How can I help you?"

"We received a call from a few panicked young ladies telling us some wild story about a man being murdered here tonight," one of them stated. "What can you tell us about that?"

Adam managed a smile, remaining calm as he spoke. "I'm afraid there's been some confusion. I didn't witness any murders here tonight. We did have a change in management, but nothing like what you're describing."

"A change in management?" the officer questioned. "I would like a word with the new manager then, please." He turned to his partner. "Wait here." The other officer nodded.

Adam escorted the police officer up the stairs and down the hall to the office. He knocked once and then opened the door.

Nika was sitting in the chair behind the desk, looking through a few ledgers spread out in front of her, appearing rather official. "Good evening, Officer," she said in a soothing tone. "Can I get you some refreshment?"

The officer smiled when he saw her. Adam suspected this was the typical reaction she got when a man first met her. She was so beautiful, and there was something incredibly serene about her tone. "No, thank you, Miss . . .?"

"Nika," she replied, standing to walk around from behind the desk, pausing for a moment when she saw delight in the officer's eyes. "I'm the manager here. What brings you by this evening?"

"I hate to disturb you, Miss Nika, but it seems a few of the young ladies who were here earlier tonight claim to have seen a dead man on the floor in this office," he stated, glancing around the room. "Any thoughts on that?"

She laughed as she continued walking over to the officer. "Honestly, I'm not surprised by such a juvenile prank," she stated, looking the man in the eyes.

"Prank?" The officer glanced over at Adam, who was standing next to the door, a stoic expression on his face.

"Yes, Officer," she answered. "The owner of this establishment hired me to be the new manager, and sadly, the previous manager was not happy about that decision. We had some words, and then I asked him to leave and to take his *women* with him. They seemed insulted by my request, so no, I'm not surprised at all by their behavior."

The officer stared at Nika for a moment. "So, where did he go?"

"Well, it seemed like he was really looking for a fight, and I didn't want any of the patrons to be disturbed by him, so I had security escort him out the back," she stated sweetly.

The officer looked at Adam, who nodded in agreement. The officer shook his head and smiled. "Well, I appreciate your time, Miss Nika. You enjoy the rest of your evening."

"Thank you, Officer. You have a good evening as well."

Adam opened the door and watched the officer walk down the hall and back downstairs. He shut the door and turned to look at his new manager.

"Thank you for your assistance, Adam," she said, walking over to him. "I appreciate your loyalty."

"You are welcome, Miss Nika."

"I wonder, do you think Mick will show me the same loyalty you have?"

"I'm not sure. Big Mick was very loyal to Mr. Rico. He appreciated the *extras* Rico had to offer."

She smiled, extending her right arm out, and placed her hand flat against his broad chest. "Is that so?" The warmth and hardness of the man's body played with her desires. "But you did not?"

"It wasn't really for me," he stated honestly. "I take care of myself."

"I can see that." Her hand slid across his chest and down his arm. "Thank you, again, Adam. That will be all."

She walked away from him, back over to the desk, and sat down as he left the office. She had found the ledger showing the illegal activities Rico had been into, and she needed to get the ledger out of the club as soon as possible. She would take it to the boss, and she hoped he would not be angry with the way she negotiated Rico's retirement. She was, after all, looking out for *his* best interests.

Nika sat back in the chair, looking around the office again. She knew exactly what she wanted to do with the space, *her* space. She would fill it with beauty, style, and elegance.

CHAPTER 25

Alexis felt restless. It was a new year, and she missed having someplace to go every day. She thought about going back to school but knew she wasn't ready yet. She started spending a lot of time at Aidan's gallery, memorizing everything, noticing whenever there were changes. The smell of the wood frames and the chemicals used to carefully clean the pieces always made her smile. She missed the world of art. It was where she belonged.

Late one afternoon, while sitting in front of a newer piece, she heard a familiar voice. She smiled when she saw Aidan approaching her. It had been a while since she had seen him.

"This is a pleasant surprise," Aidan said. "May I join you?"

"Please."

He sat down next to her. "How have you been?"

"I'm good," she responded. "Honestly, I've been feeling a bit restless lately."

He smiled. "I understand you have been spending afternoons here at the gallery."

Alexis couldn't help but laugh. "Yes, I have. I was becoming concerned they might think I was casing the place. I really miss the world of art."

"Well, I have an idea to remedy that."

"You do?"

"Miss Alexis, with your background and knowledge, I would like to offer you a position here."

"You're offering me a job? But I haven't even finished college. I don't have my degree yet."

He smiled. "I've seen enough to know you are quite knowledgeable in this world, and I would love to teach you even more . . . if you like?"

Alexis was on her feet, unable to contain her excitement. "Mr. Drake, thank you so much." She impulsively threw her arms around him when he stood, until she realized what she had done. She immediately pulled back from him, feeling a little embarrassed. "Oh, I'm so sorry, Mr. Drake . . ."

He threw his head back, laughing. "It is quite all right, and please, call me Aidan."

She looked at him, beaming with excitement. "Thank you so much, Aidan."

"Does that mean you accept my offer?" he asked, already knowing the answer. "I haven't even told you what the position is." He enjoyed teasing her, appreciating her enthusiasm.

She blushed, the tone of his voice causing her heart to flutter. "What position do you have in mind for me?"

"One of my assistants is moving on, and I need to fill the position immediately," he stated. "You would be handling phone calls, preparing purchase orders, and coordinating events and exhibits for the gallery. Is that something you would be interested in?"

"It sounds like an incredible opportunity. When would you like me to start?"

"How 'bout Monday the seventeenth?" he said, smiling at her. "You can work Monday through Friday, ten a.m. to seven p.m."

"I will be here Monday morning."

"Excellent. Come in around nine forty-five so the office manager can get all your information and the employment documents filled out."

She beamed with delight. "I can't tell you how happy I am, and I promise, you will not be disappointed."

"Oh, I know I won't be disappointed, Alexis," he replied, smiling.

Alexis left the gallery feeling like she was on top of the world. Driving to the gym to pick up Sebastian, she wondered what she was going to wear the first day. She wanted to look professional but knew she was probably going to be a little nervous too. Sounded like she would need to wear her power colors, black and garnet. She always felt like she could take on the world wearing that combination. She smiled, pulling into the parking lot of the gym. She wondered how Sebastian was going to react to the news, knowing he didn't really like Aidan.

She got out of the car and headed inside to be greeted by an empty space. It didn't really surprise her. It was Friday night, after all. Josh and Sebastian were just coming out of the locker room.

"There's my girl," Sebastian said, running over to embrace Alexis. He picked her up, spinning her around before setting her down and kissing her. "I missed you."

"I missed you too." She smiled, studying his face. "I have some great news."

"Let's hear it," he said.

"Starting Monday, I will be a new assistant at Aidan's gallery," she stated. She could tell from the look on his face, Sebastian was not as happy with the news.

He took a step back from her and looked at Josh.

"Hey, man, don't look at me," Josh responded.

"Alexis, why?" he asked.

"Because I need something to do, and I'm not ready to go back to school yet, and I miss that world," she explained, rambling on more than she intended. She stepped forward, closing the distance between them, placing her hands on his chest. "I know you don't like him, but I am so excited. Can you try being a little supportive?"

Sebastian looked down into her beautiful green eyes, seeing the sparkle he hadn't seen in months, and he relaxed, smiling when he saw her pouty bottom lip. There was no way he could say no.

"All right, I will be supportive, but you have to promise me you will be careful," he said, pulling her in close.

"I promise," she replied as she leaned forward to kiss him.

"It's the art world," Josh said, walking over to them. "I'm sure she will be fine. Besides, I've taught her well."

He pulled back from Alexis to face Josh. "You mean *we've* taught her well."

"Sure," Josh said, laughing as Sebastian punched him in the shoulder.

Alexis turned, heading for the door. "Come on, boys. I'm starving. Let's go eat."

It was Friday night and she wanted to celebrate.

CHAPTER 26

Spring was in the air, and Alexis decided to go jogging around the neighborhood. The sun was setting on a beautiful Sunday, and the temperature was perfect for sweats and a T-shirt. She closed her eyes, lifting her chin up to breathe in the freshly cut grass and flowers coming into bloom. She started out slow, getting warmed up before picking up her pace. She enjoyed jogging because it gave her the opportunity to think and clear her head.

She had a lot on her mind lately. She had been working at the gallery for a few months now and couldn't be happier. Aidan came in a few times a week, usually towards the end of the day to look over any new acquisitions. He seemed quite pleased with her work and how well she fit in with the rest of the team. Her salary was nice, although she didn't really need the money. She was thrilled to have a purpose in life again, well, a purpose she could share with everybody.

She still had not really spoken with Nika since their conversation on Thanksgiving. After Nika was so dismissive and uncaring about what happened to Gram, she was beginning to wonder if there was a friendship left between them. Thankfully, Maxi had been spending a lot of time at the gym training, so the two of them were sparring and hanging out a lot. It was nice having a female friend in her life again. The guys were great, but sometimes she just needed some girl time.

Alexis could tell Maxi's crush on Josh was growing every time she watched the two of them sparring. It wasn't so much what she observed, but more what she felt coming off the young girl in waves. Maxi was right about Alexis's empathic powers becoming stronger now that she was training more. Alexis still couldn't seem to get any kind of reading off Josh, for herself or Maxi. His demeanor indicated Maxi was like a little sister to him, and Alexis couldn't see that changing in the future. The man was like a blank canvas most of the time, which made it easier for Alexis, now knowing how he really felt about her.

Maxi had come over a few times, and she and Alexis would head down to the basement to read and share how they felt about the incredible gifts they had been given.

"Mine still doesn't seem to be that great of a gift," Maxi stated. "*Tracker*, I mean other than having the ability to sense somebody's intentions, what am I really going to do with it?"

"Are you kidding?" Alexis asked. "When was the last time you lost something?"

They both laughed. "My tracking ability is more for finding people rather than inanimate objects."

"Still," Alexis began, "becoming a badass fighter? Pretty damn cool."

"Oh yeah, that part is completely awesome."

Alexis picked up her pace a bit as she began running up a hill. She could feel a difference in her strength and endurance level from all the training she had been doing lately. Her mind wandered to everything she had accomplished recently. She was becoming very proficient with all her abilities. She'd even caught Josh off guard a few times, which immediately prompted a happy dance around the ring. He just laughed at her, letting her have her moment. Then he would remind her why she should never let her guard down, usually in the form of her getting pinned.

Moving through the neighborhood, Alexis found her thoughts going to Aidan. He was so knowledgeable and sophisticated, which really intrigued her. She never heard him speak of his personal life, and she often wondered if he had ever been married. Did he have any children? They had spent a lot of time together recently, going over new pieces for the gallery, and he always asked her opinion, expressing how much he valued her input.

Looking around, she noticed she was at the upper end of the neighborhood, where all the expensive houses were located. She stopped in front of one to admire it. It was the most elegant house she had ever seen in her life, and it was huge. She could tell the exterior had been altered. The lines of the original house were still easy to see, but there had been extensive remodeling and updates done to it recently, including a gambrel roof. Maybe the new owner had purchased the lot next to the house to expand it. She could only imagine what the interior looked like, and she was sure the view from the top floor was to die for.

She didn't realize how long she had been staring at the magnificent house and its incredible landscaping when she heard a familiar voice that made her spin around.

"Alexis, what brings you to my neighborhood?" Aidan asked.

"Your neighborhood?"

"Yes," he replied. "As a matter of fact, my doorstep. This is where I live."

"This is your house?"

"Yes, it is," he stated proudly. "Would you like to come in? You can finally see my private collection."

Alexis began looking around the neighborhood. "I guess I could come in for a minute."

"Is there somewhere else you need to be?"

"No, not until tomorrow morning," she declared, laughing.

"I can drive you home afterward," he stated.

"Okay," she replied, following him up the stairs to the front door. She knew Sebastian would not be happy if he knew she was going to be alone with Aidan in his home, but then again, why worry him?

Aidan opened the front door, allowing Alexis to enter first, her eyes trying to take everything in at once. The décor of the entryway was wonderfully warm with wood accents on the walls and the banister leading upstairs. The inlaid floors had a distinct pattern in a darker wood around the perimeter, and there was a lovely settee off to the side just as you entered the space. The smell of the wood filled the air, offering a warm and inviting feel combined with old-world charm.

"Your home is beautiful, Aidan," she stated. Straight ahead in the entry was a library table hosting a collection of candle holders and a few wood carvings. The table was flanked by a pair of oversized love seats in dark leather upholstery. Over the library table was a portrait, a painting of a man who had to be a distant relative. "This portrait is wonderful. Is it your grandfather? The resemblance is uncanny."

He smiled. "The traits run quite strong in my family."

"I'll say," she managed, unable to take her eyes off the image. "Would you mind if I used your powder room?"

"Of course. It's the first door on the right," he said, gesturing just past another settee in the entryway.

Once inside the bathroom, Alexis flipped the light on to get a look at herself in the mirror. She rolled her eyes and sighed, seeing her reflection. She splashed some water on her face and ran her wet hands down her arms to wipe away any perspiration. She wiped her hands on her sweats and then pulled the hair tie out of her hair, leaving it on her wrist. She ran her fingers through her hair to fluff it up a bit. She wasn't sure why she was so concerned about her appearance suddenly. Still, he was her boss, and this was the first time in his home.

She opened the door and was greeted immediately by Aidan. "Would you like a tour?" he asked.

"Yes, please," she replied, still looking around. She couldn't get over all the tapestries and ornate rugs that adorned his home. His collection was quite impressive, yet somehow the house didn't feel like a museum. Instead, it was very inviting.

"This piece I picked up a few years back," he announced, lingering in front of the fireplace in the living room. "The original owner wasn't sure if he wanted to part with it, but I managed to persuade him."

"Oil on canvas, right?" She studied the brushstrokes and the figures in the painting. A man on horseback with a woman entrapped under his arm, while another man held her in place. "The colors are so rich and vibrant."

"I knew I hired you for a reason," he announced proudly. "Would you like a glass of wine?"

She watched Aidan walk across the room to a bar area to pour himself a glass of red wine, another glass at the ready. "Yes, thank you."

She slowly made her way around the living room, pausing to study each piece hanging on the wall. She had a feeling every one of them had an interesting story of how it was acquired.

"Shall we sit?" He handed her the glass of wine, and she followed him over to the large sofa. She took a sip, noticing the smooth yet full body of the merlot. An art book on the coffee table caught her attention, and she couldn't help but get excited.

"I have always wanted a copy of this book," she said, setting her wine down so she could pick up the large book with both hands.

"It depicts a wonderful collection," Aidan stated. "I'm surprised you do not have a copy."

"Well, it's very popular." She turned each page carefully. "Every time I look for it at the bookstore, it's sold out and on back-order. I enjoy reading about art and its origins as much as I love viewing the finished pieces."

Aidan smiled and stood with his wine. "Come with me then. I must show you where I spend a lot of my time when I'm at home."

She set the book down and picked up her glass, following him out of the living room. They walked up three flights of stairs until they reached what would normally be a boring attic in any other house. In Aidan's, it was a spectacular library, the walls and ceiling covered in rich wood paneling, like the paneling downstairs. The natural angles of the roofline offered additional warmth, making the seating area straight across from the staircase feel even more inviting. The perimeter of the room was lined with bookshelves, and there had to be hundreds of books in his collection, many which looked to be first editions. She walked slowly along the bookshelves, her eyes gathering as many titles as possible, while her fingertips gently caressed the spines.

"Aidan, your collection is quite impressive."

He smiled, taking a seat in one of the chairs in the seating area. "Feel free to select one you would like to borrow."

She was dumbfounded. How could she possibly choose from this collection? She laughed, walking over to the other chair where he was sitting. "I don't know how I will ever decide. It's better than going to a library." She sat down and took another sip of wine, looking around the room. "This space is so inviting and comfortable."

"Thank you. I'm glad you like it."

Aidan spoke about his various collections, and Alexis noticed she was feeling a bit lightheaded. She probably needed to eat something. She took another sip of wine before carefully setting the glass down on the small nest of tables between them. She was finding it more and more difficult to focus on his words, the sound of his voice becoming more mesmerizing the longer he spoke. Her body felt heavy, like she was unable to move. She looked at him, and she could see he was speaking, but she was unable to hear what he was saying. Instead, all she could do was focus on his smile and his face. Then, she was gone.

Alexis woke to find herself naked, a cool breeze flowing over the top of her body. She was lying on a bed; her mouth was dry and her head foggy. The foot of the bed shifted a bit from the weight of another person, and as she tried to lift her head, she found she couldn't move. She felt extremely heavy, and everything seemed to be moving in slow motion. She inhaled sharply when she felt a pair of lips on her right ankle, leaving a trail of kisses as they made their way up the length of her leg. Straining to lift her head, she saw it was Aidan. He smiled as she watched his strong naked body crawling towards her. She knew she shouldn't be here, but she didn't want to leave. She just wanted him.

"Sweet Alexis," he whispered, gazing into her half-closed eyes. "Tell me what you want, and it shall be yours."

She managed to find the strength to lift her right hand up, placing her fingertips on his cheek. He felt cold and hard, like marble, but his lips were full and inviting. "I want you," she said with hunger. "I want *you*, Aidan."

"Are you sure, my dear?" He smiled down at her, his face inches from hers.

"Yes, yes please," she responded in an urgent whisper.

He stroked her face with his fingertips, softly tracing her lower jawline, before reaching for a handful of her hair. "As you wish." He leaned down, lifting her head at the same time to capture her hungry mouth with his own. He kissed her passionately, and she felt like she couldn't breathe, but she didn't care. She wanted him. She needed him. His lips finally left hers, making their way down to encircle her left nipple. She closed her eyes and cried out as she felt a bit of pain from his teeth, her fingertips digging into his strong shoulders. Her body ached to be sated from his touch. It felt like his mouth was everywhere, all over her body, stirring emotions she had never felt before. She couldn't get enough.

It felt like he was in control of everything, only allowing her to move when *he* wanted. His hands caressed her hips and thighs, and she cried out again when she felt his tongue on the inside of her right thigh followed by a sharp pain. Her eyes felt heavy, like they might close forever, as a sense of calm came over her mind. She felt a warm liquid spilling down her lips from above. She opened her eyes enough to see Aidan holding his wrist over her mouth. There was something dark smeared across his lips.

"Drink, Alexis," his voice hissed. "DRINK!"

She lifted her head, wrapping her lips around the opening in his skin. She closed her eyes, drinking in every ounce of the metallic elixir, holding his arm to her mouth with a newfound strength. When the last drop hit the back of her throat, his body covered hers as he drove himself deep inside her. She cried out once more before his demanding mouth found hers, feeling revived for a moment, like she was suddenly reborn. She could move now. She lifted her arms up, clinging to him, wrapping her leg around his waist like she was afraid to let go. Her body peaked, and she screamed in the night before she was gone.

CHAPTER 27

Sebastian was worried. It was late Tuesday afternoon, and he couldn't reach Alexis. He had called her house, leaving a few messages after he called the gallery Monday afternoon. Trish at the gallery said Alexis never showed up to work that morning and she had not called in either. It wasn't like Alexis to be out of touch for so long, especially missing work. She really loved her new job, and he was thrilled to see her happy again.

He drove to her house, knocking on the door several times before using his key to let himself in. Entering the dark house, he knew something was wrong because there were no lights on anywhere, which was completely out of character for her. She always had at least one or two on, even if it was just the light on the range hood.

He moved quietly through the house, checking all the rooms downstairs, finding nothing out of place, so he headed upstairs to her room. The door was closed, and he couldn't hear any noise coming from inside. He knocked softly, listening for a response.

Nothing. Slowly he opened the door and entered the room. It was extremely dark since the curtains were closed completely, making it difficult to see.

"Alexis?" he whispered. Maybe she was sick, in a deep sleep. He found his way over to the bed, feeling around until his right hand found a body lying under the sheets, cold to the touch through the sheet. He quickly reached for the lamp on the nightstand, turning it on. She was completely covered up. He hesitated for a moment before pulling the top sheet back to reveal her head and face. She looked so pale yet somehow peaceful. *Shit!*

"Alexis!" he called, shaking her. No response. "Alexis, wake up!" Still no response. He reached for the phone on the nightstand, dialing the gym. He hoped Josh was in his office.

"Hello?"

"Josh, it's Sebastian. I need you to come over to Alexis's house right away. There's something wrong with her. The front door is unlocked."

"On my way," Josh replied.

Sebastian stared at the handset for a moment before hanging it up. He loved that about Josh. He didn't waste time with unnecessary questions that could be answered later. He just responded.

He directed his attention back to Alexis. She still had not moved. He pulled the covers down further to reveal she was not wearing any clothes, and her entire body was incredibly pale and cold. He needed to warm her up.

He moved quickly to the bathroom, turning the water on in the shower. He removed his clothes down to his underwear and walked back to get her, when he saw it. *No. It can't be.* Shaking his head, he picked her up and carried her into the bathroom, carefully stepping over the edge of the bathtub with her. He knew Josh would be there soon, but there was no time for modesty. He held Alexis in his arms as the warm water poured down over her body, reflecting on the last time they were there together, their bath time. He stared at her face, caressing her cheek, gently kissing her lips. No breath. No pulse. No response at all until the increasing heat from the water started warming her skin, and then she moaned softly. He shifted, setting her legs down. He pressed his body against hers, against the tile wall behind her. He reached out, readjusting the temperature of the water again, making it as hot as he could stand.

"Sebastian!" Josh called.

"Up here, in the bathroom!" he replied. "Please, Alexis, wake up, baby!"

"What the hell happened?" Josh asked from the doorway.

"I don't know," he replied. "When I got here, I found her in bed, cold as ice and unresponsive."

"Should I call an ambulance?" Josh asked, wondering why his friend had not already done so.

"They can't help," he stated, not bothering to look at his friend.

Josh stared at his friend for a moment. There was something in his voice he had never heard before, genuine fear.

"Sebastian, what the hell is going on?" Josh demanded.

"I think . . ." he began. "I think Alexis was bitten by a vampire." Sebastian turned his head, staring at his friend, a mix of fear and despair on his face.

"Holy shit," Josh said quietly. "What makes you think . . .?"

"When I found her, she was naked, and I saw two puncture wounds on her inner thigh." Alexis moaned again, and Sebastian looked at her. He leaned forward, kissing her forehead, her skin still so cold to the touch. She opened her eyes a little, trying to focus on him. "Alexis!"

"Sebastian?" she whispered. "What's happening?"

"Alexis, you're sick, but Josh and I are going to help you, okay?"

"I'm so . . . hungry." Her voice was raspy and her lips dry. "My body feels strange."

"I know, baby. Let's get you dried off and dressed," he gently said. "Josh, can you hand me that towel?" He nodded his chin towards the rack on the wall. Josh handed him the towel, then reached in the shower to turn off the water, noticing how red his friend's skin was.

Sebastian dried her off, wrapping the towel around her body, which still felt cold. "Josh, can you help her out of the shower?"

Josh took a step forward to support her as she stepped out. She didn't have much balance, leaning into his body. Her wet hair soaked his shirt as her head fell to his chest, and she sniffed him.

"You smell good," she whispered, desire flowing across the air.

"Um, Sebastian?"

"I know man," Sebastian responded. "I'm hurrying."

Sebastian dried himself off quickly, removing his underwear before tying a towel around his waist. He grabbed a robe for Alexis off the back of the door and draped it over her shoulders before pulling the wet towel off her. He helped her guide her arms into the sleeves and tied the robe closed while Josh steadied her from behind.

"If she was bitten, she will need to feed," Josh stated plainly, stepping aside so Sebastian could guide her through the doorway.

"I know," he replied, maneuvering her down the hall to her room. "I'll go out and get something. I need you to stay here with her."

"Why do I feel like I just drew the short straw?" Josh asked, following them down the hall.

Sebastian glanced at him over his shoulder. "You're the only one who can subdue her if she gets . . ."

"*Really* hungry?" Josh asked in a mocking tone.

"Josh," Sebastian began, "I trust you. You are the only one who can handle her. Please."

"I'm sorry," Josh said. "Go, I've got this."

Sebastian stepped aside so Josh could lead Alexis to her bed, assisting her as she placed a knee on the edge before crawling towards the headboard. She leaned against it and pulled her knees up to her chest, her eyes partially open. Josh pulled the covers up to her chin, tucking them in tight around her body. She sat there, staring up at the ceiling through half-closed eyes for a few moments. Finally, she closed them completely and moaned softly. *She was so hungry.*

Sebastian pulled on some sweats and a shirt he found in one of the dresser drawers, watching her the entire time. "I'm out of here."

"Just hurry," Josh said, staring at his friend.

"I will," he replied, slipping his shoes on and walking quickly out of the bedroom and down the hall.

Josh heard the front door shut, and as he looked back at Alexis, he knew he didn't have long before her hunger would really become a problem, for both of them. He pulled a chair over from the desk, keeping an eye on her the entire time. He placed the chair between the bed and the door of the bedroom. He sat down, watching her as she watched him.

He knew the sun was almost down without having to look out the window. He had been trained for a lot of things, but this was not one of them. He had learned about so many things in the last few months he never would have believed to be real, but magic and vampires *were* real.

"Josh?" she asked in a soft voice, looking back up at the ceiling. "Where did Sebastian go?"

"He's running an errand and will be back soon."

"So we are all alone?" Her head fell to the side as she watched him, her sleepy eyes staring deep into his.

"We are for the moment, yes." He could tell she was struggling.

She continued watching him, studying him, her eyes focusing on the pulse on the side of his neck. She was making him uncomfortable, and she was enjoying it. She could smell his desire for her. Maxi was right. There was nothing he could hide from her now.

"Josh?"

"Yes, Alexis."

"I need you," she purred as she began peeling back the covers, her robe in disarray as she pulled her legs out, exposing her flawless pale skin. She placed her feet on the floor and continued watching him. She pulled at the sides of her robe, allowing the material to slip off her shoulders, revealing her bare breasts. She could smell his excitement and feel his pulse quicken, like a buzz across her skin, making her more excited. "I know you want me. You've *always* wanted me, Josh."

"Alexis," he said, standing and picking up the chair to set it aside. "You need to cover yourself up and get back in bed. Sebastian will be back soon, and then you will feel better."

"But *you* have what I need to feel better, and you're here now," she said, her hands reaching down to pull the lower half of her robe apart. She closed her eyes a bit, her mouth falling open to reveal her long fangs. Her eyes changed to a translucent green, and she moaned when she heard his pulse quicken, smiling.

"Alexis, please," he pleaded. She was so beautiful, even now. He felt like he was being pulled towards her.

She stood up slowly, allowing her robe to fall to the floor, pleased as his eyes fell to the flatness of her stomach and the curve of her hips. She took a step towards him, her hands gently caressing her breasts. The tips of her fingernails traced the outline of her nipples and turned them hard in an instant. He took a step back, his heart pounding in his chest with excitement.

"It can just be our little secret," she purred through pouty lips, her eyes fixed on his. "I won't tell if you won't."

He sighed. "Okay."

She smiled, taking another step forward, only to be met with a left hook. She fell back on the bed, out cold. Josh sighed, staring down at her beautiful naked body lying across the bed, the feminine curve of her hips and buttocks holding his attention longer than they should. He slowly walked forward, carefully tucking her back into bed, securing her hands behind her back with the tie from her robe. He knew it wasn't much, but he needed to get her covered back up. It was going to be difficult enough explaining to Sebastian why she was naked again. He picked up the chair and placed it back in between the bed and the door. He sat down, leaning forward with his elbows balanced on his knees, watching and waiting.

Ten minutes later the front door opened and Sebastian raced up the stairs. Josh moved the chair out of the way as Sebastian entered the room carrying a bag. Sebastian looked at his friend, and then his eyes went to Alexis lying in bed all covered up, the robe on the floor. Sebastian looked back at his friend, puzzled.

"Josh?" he began. "What happened?"

"She got *hungry*." Sebastian stared at him, waiting for the rest of the explanation. "Then she tried to seduce me."

Sebastian glanced back at Alexis on the bed, noticing a bruise on her right cheek. "So you knocked her out?" he asked, turning back towards Josh.

"I'm sorry," Josh began. "It was either that or *feed* her."

"Shit! You okay, man?"

"Yeah, I'm good," he replied calmly. "We should probably feed her now."

"Agreed." He handed the bag to Josh before walking over to the bed. He picked up the robe while Josh set the bag down on the desk, his back to them. Josh carefully removed a large Styrofoam container with a lid from the bag, noticing there were at least three more inside and a couple of straws.

He heard Sebastian behind him probably doing whatever he needed to do to make sure Alexis was covered up again. Although, after all the times Josh had fantasized about her, nothing would remove the image of her naked body now burned in his brain. She was even more beautiful than he had imagined.

"Okay," Sebastian said. "Come on over."

He turned to find Sebastian sitting behind Alexis, her body leaning back against him, trying to bring her back around. She stirred and lunged forward when she saw Josh. Sebastian struggled, holding on to her arms when she picked up the scent from the blood.

"Alexis, it's okay," he whispered in her ear. "We have what you need."

Josh moved forward slowly, holding the container of blood in front of him. He had poked a hole in the lid to slide a straw through. Her translucent eyes were locked on the container, and she hissed at him, revealing her fangs, saliva dripping from their razor-sharp tips. He slowly sat down on the edge of the bed and extended the container out towards her. She wrapped her lips around the straw, quickly draining the contents. When she was done, she released the straw from her lips and leaned back against Sebastian like a satisfied kitten. She closed her eyes and sighed. Josh watched as the bruise on her cheek slowly disappeared. *She feeds, she heals. Neat trick.*

Josh looked at Sebastian. "So now what?"

"I'm not sure," Sebastian replied. "I've got to find out what happened and who did this to her. Alexis?" Sebastian whispered, shaking her a bit.

"Mm," she replied, her eyes still closed as she pressed her body into his warmth.

"Alexis, what do you remember about the last couple of days?"

She stirred, her eyes opening wider than before. "Oh, Josh!" she exclaimed. "I'm so sorry. I'm so embarrassed."

Josh smiled. "It's okay, Alexis. I've had worse days."

"Alexis, what is the last thing you remember?" Sebastian asked.

"I went jogging Sunday afternoon," she replied. "Late Sunday afternoon. That's it. Why? What day is it?"

"It's Tuesday night," Josh stated.

The look on her face said it all. She suddenly felt lost and confused. "This can't be happening." She pulled away from Sebastian and was suddenly standing by the window. The men looked at each other, shocked by the speed of her movements. She pulled the curtain back to see it was nighttime. She turned and looked at Sebastian and then Josh. "Am I really a vampire? Did I really just drink *blood*?"

Sebastian climbed off the bed, slowly walking towards her, while Josh stood up and put some distance between them. He needed to be ready for whatever might happen next.

"Yes, you are a vampire," Sebastian said.

Anger filled her as she backed away from him, sliding along the wall, wedging her body into the corner. "Please, stay back. I don't feel like I have a lot of control right now, and I don't want to hurt you."

Sebastian stopped moving. "Alexis, try and remember what happened while you were jogging."

She reached up and adjusted her robe, suddenly feeling extremely modest, not that it really mattered. Both men in the room had already seen her naked, only one of whom she was dating. *Damn!*

She pushed her wet hair back from her face. Her brow furrowed, becoming contorted and strained as she tried to reflect on the past events. "It was a beautiful afternoon, surprisingly warm. I remember the smell of freshly cut grass and . . ." She stopped talking, her eyes widening, searching for more information, her face filled with confusion. "DAMN IT! Why can't I remember?" Suddenly, she looked like a wild animal, trapped, with a great need to escape. "Lorcan McCowan! He must have found me!" She looked at Sebastian, feeling her eyes change again, and she bared her teeth, growling at both as more rage filled her.

"Alexis," Sebastian began, "we don't know anything for sure, but we will figure this out. Try and focus on something else."

She closed her eyes and relaxed, and when she opened them again, they were back to normal. She could feel every pulse in the room slowing down. *Good*, she thought. They weren't calling to her like before.

"I need to put some clothes on," she stated, reaching up and adjusting her robe again. The men looked at each other. "I promise I will not jump out the window. I just need some clothes."

"Okay," Sebastian said. "We'll be out in the hall."

The two men stepped out of the room, and a few moments later Alexis joined them. She seemed calmer, normal, if that was possible after just finding out you had been turned into a vampire.

"I need to go to the basement." She walked into her grandmother's room, and the guys followed. "There has to be a way to track him down."

She leaned down, pulling on the lock on the front of the chest, but it wouldn't open. She pulled a little harder this time, but the lock still wouldn't release. Frustrated, she pulled as hard as she could, breaking the lock and dropping the remains on the floor. She quickly opened the chest and saw clothing. Dropping to her knees, she pawed through the chest of clothing like a dog unearthing a bone it had buried, as both men watched. It was gone. The ladder and landing were gone. She sat back on her heels, her head falling back as she screamed in frustration, a single tear rolling down her cheek. She closed her eyes and tried to regain her composure. Sebastian and Josh stood watching, not knowing what to do. Suddenly she was on her feet running past them. Fortunately, Sebastian knew where she was headed.

Her speed was undeniable. She was in the study pushing her favorite childhood book against the back of the bookshelf before they even entered the room. Her frustration grew with each failed attempt, and all they could do was watch.

Alexis let out a piercing cry of frustration, the sharp tone filling the small room as she swept her arms across the shelves and sent all the books onto the floor. Sebastian started to take a step forward, when Josh grabbed his arm, pulling him back as more books flew across the room. They exchanged a look of concern.

Alexis turned to look at them, defeat exuding from every pore. Her face was dark, her eyes even darker. The light that had once resonated from this beautiful young woman was gone. She turned away from them and walked over to the window, gazing out into the night, to what was now *her* world.

"Alexis," Sebastian called softly. "Please look at me."

"Go," she said, her voice low, full of despair.

"I'm not leaving you," he replied. "I love you."

She spun around and stared at the face of the man she was meant to spend the rest of her life with. "How can you love me? I'm supposed to be a healer and a protector. Now I'm a goddamn predator!"

"Alexis, please," Sebastian pleaded. "We will figure this out."

"You don't understand," she began, looking at the two men. "I am a killer now. I would kill both of you if I had not already fed. It's in my nature." Suddenly, she erupted with laughter, their nervous tension dancing across her tongue like a divine elixir. "Hey, Josh, wanna see who's more of a badass now?" Her smile was genuine, as was the dark meaning behind it.

"No." He already knew the answer.

Her smile faded as a look of regret crossed her face. "I'm sorry, I'm so sorry," she said to both men, running her hands through her half-dried hair. "I feel like I'm being torn apart. I need to learn how to control this."

"That's my girl," Sebastian said.

"Maybe approach it like the skills you learned for healing and psychokinesis," Josh suggested. "Learn to focus your energy to control the darkness within you."

She smiled. "Thank you, Josh."

"In the meantime, we need to make sure you always have blood in the house," Sebastian stated. "It's too early for you to be put in the position of trying to control your hunger."

"Agreed," Alexis said.

"I'm sure we can pick up blood from a number of the local butcher shops," Josh offered.

"Exactly," Sebastian replied, watching Alexis to see her response. She seemed pleased with the idea. "I doubt they will ask any questions about our needs, especially if we pay enough."

"We can do it in shifts," Josh stated. "I've got a few near me I can bounce between."

"Good, and I saw a few just down the way from here," Sebastian added.

"Thanks, guys. So how do I get my memory back?"

Sebastian slowly took a step closer to her, watching her face and eyes. He knew she was still extremely dangerous, but all he wanted to do was hold her.

She looked up into Sebastian's eyes, her own filling with tears. She wanted nothing more than to be wrapped in his arms for comfort, well, almost nothing more. The pulse in his neck caught her attention again, and tears fell as she closed her eyes, squeezing them tight. She knew he had stopped moving forward because she no longer heard shoes shuffling across the hardwood floor. All her senses were more acute now.

"Alexis?"

She opened her eyes to find Sebastian smiling at her, his unconditional love causing even more tears to spill down her cheeks.

"I promise, we are going to figure this out," he stated, slowly reaching up to brush her tears away. His hand felt hot against her cool skin.

"Thank you."

"Alexis, we are going to find Lorcan McCowan and take care of him," Josh declared.

"Thank you, both of you. You should probably go. I feel like being alone right now. I need to wrap my head around everything and make a few calls, see if Margaret or somebody else in the coven can help me."

"What about my mom?" Sebastian asked.

Alexis dropped her eyes a moment, and she looked back up at him. They were filled with despair. "No, I feel like she would be disappointed in me now. Please don't tell her."

"Okay," Sebastian replied softly. He instinctively stepped forward to kiss her good-bye, stopping a few feet away. "I love you."

"I love you too."

Alexis stood in the study, watching as the two most important men in her life headed towards the front door. She sat down in a chair near the bookshelves, cringing when she heard the door close. She glanced down at the floor, at the books from the shelves scattered across the room. *What a mess*. Sliding to the edge of the chair, she knelt in the floor, reaching for the books, and made small stacks to be moved back up to the shelves. She was oddly relieved with the project she had created for herself. This would give her time to think and calm down. Josh was right. Lorcan McCowan would pay.

CHAPTER 28

The following weeks were even more difficult in some ways than when Alexis lost Gram. At least after Gram was gone, she still had something that resembled a normal existence. Now, it was anything but normal. Sleeping all day and being awake all night would have been fine if she had a job working the night shift. That would make sense. Nothing made sense now. Hell, she couldn't even go to the bank. Thankfully, she had some cash in the house for any *supplies* she might need. Sebastian and Josh would stop by during the day to drop things off while she was sleeping. Sebastian would leave her notes, a few times asking her if she had any memory about that Sunday. She didn't. She had no idea why Lorcan McCowan had done this to her, why he had not just killed her. Something was preventing her from remembering everything.

Alexis called Margaret, leaving messages for her to please call her back. When she finally did, it was to inform Alexis she was not to contact her or any other member of the coven again.

They didn't want anyone else lost to the evil she had become. Frustrated, Alexis spent hours sitting on the floor upstairs in her grandmother's room, next to the chest, meditating to spark her memory. She couldn't get to the basement, but part of her believed being close to it might help her draw power to find the answers she was looking for. She couldn't find her memories, but she was learning how to control her hunger and the desire to kill. She took it as a win.

Alexis had called the gallery late Wednesday afternoon apologizing for not showing up or calling earlier. She told Trish, the office manager, she had become terribly ill suddenly and was not sure when or if she would be coming back to work. Trish thanked her for the call and let Alexis know she would break the news to Aidan. Aidan. She felt like she had let him down and wished she could call him personally and apologize.

Alexis spent her nights wandering through the house, feeling isolated and trapped since she couldn't go outside. She had talked it over with the guys one night, and everybody agreed it was too soon for her to mix with the public. She continued to try accessing the basement, but it just wasn't there. No trace of any magic or her heritage was left in the house. She also discovered she could no longer touch the locket Gram had given her, as it caused burning and blistering across her fingertips when she tried. It was meant to protect against evil, which was what she was now. According to the universe, her bloodline was completely gone.

One night, out of desperation, she called Claire just to hear a friendly familiar voice. Claire apologized, telling Alexis she didn't hold her responsible for what had happened to her; however, the coven made it clear that no one was to be near her or associate with her. How the hell did the coven even know? Sebastian and Josh were her only real links to the outside world, and nobody was going to tell Sebastian he couldn't see Alexis.

She continued practicing her meditation and focus drills, approaching her new existence from a logical angle. It was the only way she was going to find some level of peace. She knew she would never be the same now that she was a vampire, but she was determined to not become a monster.

After weeks of being cooped up in the house, Alexis asked the guys to take a walk with her. She needed a change of scenery, to get some fresh air and test her control. She missed spending time with them, and it made things seem more normal for her to be around humans. She made it a point to quell her hunger before leaving the house, especially since this was the first time she was going to be around people other than Sebastian and Josh.

The guys showed up just after the sun went down on a Friday night. Alexis opened the door, stepping outside for the first time in what seemed like a lifetime. Well, technically it was. Her human life was over, and her existence had changed. The world looked and felt completely different now. Ironically, in some ways, she never felt more alive. She could hear and smell everything. Her senses were primed for the hunt, but instead, she focused on things around her that she had never really noticed before. Oil residue built up on the street or the heavy fragrance of freshly applied perfume, some of which should be used more sparingly. Some smells made it more of a challenge to stay in control, like the neighbor who cut her finger slicing tomatoes for that evening's salad. Alexis caught a glimpse of her standing at the sink running cold water over her wound. This was a good test for her though.

Alexis changed several window coverings in the house, allowing her to move more freely no matter what time of day it was. She had also called Mr. Blake's office, leaving several messages stating she needed to schedule a meeting with him. Every evening she would check for return calls when she got up, but nothing ever came in. She needed to find out what her options were for liquidating some assets like the cars and perhaps the house. Her thoughts about selling the house were mixed, but she needed a change. There were just too many memories from her previous life, a life that was gone forever.

One night, just after the sun went down, she went out for a walk and found herself downtown near Mr. Blake's office. She went upstairs hoping she would run into him. She was told he was not in, but his answering service was available.

"I have left several messages for Mr. Blake to call me, and I would like to schedule a meeting with him," she told the service.

"I'm sorry, but Mr. Blake has been working on a big case for a client," the woman stated.

Alexis could feel her impatience rising. "*I'm* a client."

"Your name?"

"McBain, Alexis."

The woman's eyes focused on her for a moment and then quickly looked away. The woman's heart was beating faster, the pounding filling Alexis's head. Fear trickled across the air in the office, pleasing Alexis. She leaned over the counter, her eyes focusing on the woman's face, trying to ignore the rapid pulse in her neck. "Is there something wrong?"

"No, no, nothing at all," the woman managed to say, struggling to look up. "I will tell Mr. Blake you came by to see him."

She turned away from the woman and walked to the elevator to push the button. Turning to glance back at the woman now busying herself with paperwork, Alexis heard Mr. Blake's voice coming from behind his closed door. She closed her eyes, the smell of him filling her senses. He was there, but he was avoiding her. Stepping onto the elevator, she heard him say he was just now leaving the office.

Alexis couldn't imagine why Blake had been avoiding her calls or why his service told her he had already left. She decided to let it go for the moment, but she needed to get things figured out soon. She was going to sell the house. She needed a place of her own, perhaps somewhere inside the city. A high-rise would be nice, something up off the ground, making her a little more difficult to reach. She still wanted windows, more like *needed* windows, with something over them to protect her during the day like she had now.

Alexis contacted a real estate agent the next morning, letting the agent know she wanted to sell the house. The agent was excited about the new listing and believed it would sell quickly due to the location and its condition. Gram had maintained it well. Every time Alexis would get a call from the agent to say she had somebody interested in the house, another call would come in shortly thereafter saying they'd had a change of heart. Once or twice, she could understand, but it had been a few weeks now, and nobody had kept their appointment to view the house. Something or someone was interfering, and Alexis had an idea who. She just couldn't figure out why.

Alexis still had not heard from Nika, zero contact. The more time that passed without hearing from her, the less she cared. Her emotions, or rather her lack of humanity, really helped zero in on what was important to her now. Feeding. Surviving. Maintaining control. There were times she was surprised how connected she still felt to Sebastian and Josh. Guessed it was more like an alliance. Still, she knew the day would come when she would find out exactly what Nika had been up to.

CHAPTER 29

Nika was bored, and that was never a good thing. She was frustrated since the club was under construction. She needed to have some fun, so she decided to try something new and different.

She walked down the sidewalk to a bus stop, the sunset filling the sky with bright shades of burnt orange and pink, a few tufts of smoky clouds hovering across the palette. She was the only one standing at the stop, and as the bus approached her, she smiled to herself. This was going to be different, especially since she had never ridden in any public transportation before. She was more of a car service, limo kind of girl.

The bus stopped, and a few people got off as she got on. She smiled at the driver as she dropped her money into the slot. She walked slowly down the aisle towards the back of the bus, the long seat spanning the width offering her a perfect spot in the middle. There were only a few people left on board. She had selected her dress well. It was black, making her pale skin even more striking with her flaming curls. The skirt was longer than what she normally wore, flowing nicely as she moved. It also allowed her to conceal or reveal anything she wanted. She noticed the driver watching her, so she smiled, and he smiled back as he continued driving the bus down the street. He looked to be in his early thirties, full of life. Just what she liked. She casually crossed her legs as she looked out the window, taking in the scenery as it passed by, and she waited.

Ten minutes later, the sun was completely down as the last person got off the bus. Nika looked down the aisle towards the front to find the driver watching her, and she smiled again. Shifting her body slightly, she slid down in the seat just a little and slowly uncrossed her legs. She placed her feet on the floor, shoulder width apart, and laid her hands flat on her skirt. She began sliding the material higher and higher up the length of her legs, watching the driver watch her. He seemed shocked and surprised, glancing back at the road, knowing he needed to find a secluded spot. He couldn't believe what was happening, but he knew he wanted to be a part of it.

A few moments later, the driver maneuvered the bus under an overpass, switching the sign to "Out of Service." He dimmed the lights on the inside of the bus and unfastened his seat belt, watching her in the mirror above his head. She now had her skirt pulled all the way up, draped across her thighs, the straps of her black garter belt visible where they attached to her stockings. She placed a foot on the seats in front of her on either side of the aisle, and he could see she was wearing pink panties.

He slowly got out of his seat and walked down the aisle, stopping just a few feet from her. The closer he got, the stronger he smelled, a mix of sweat, cologne, and excitement.

"What's your name?" she asked sweetly, studying him.

"Sam." His mouth was suddenly very dry.

"I'm Nika."

He watched her tongue glide slowly along her bottom lip.

"Hey, Sam, do you want to have some fun?"

He couldn't believe what he was hearing. "Yes, I do," he replied.

She placed her feet, one at a time, back down on the floor. She stood, holding the skirt of her dress against the tops of her thighs, and Sam was mesmerized, frozen in place. She let go of her skirt, and he watched as the fabric spilled down towards the floor. She extended her left arm out, and he took her hand. She pulled him towards her, turning him before gently pushing him down in the seat. She stood over him, and he watched her, his pulse racing even more when she put her left foot up on the seat on the outside of his leg. She pulled the fabric of her skirt up, again draping it over her leg. His eyes stared back into hers as he slowly reached up with his right hand, caressing the exposed skin on her inner thigh. It was cool to the touch yet so soft and smooth, like silk.

She watched him through half-closed eyes, pushing her hips out towards him as he reached his hand underneath her long skirt, past her garter strap. She moaned when she felt the warmth of his fingers push past the fabric of her panties. She allowed him to explore her a few moments, pleasure building up in her, and when she heard his belt being pulled apart, she pushed his hand aside, moving forward to straddle his lap. Kissing him deeply, she could feel his hands underneath her, adjusting for what was to come. She sat down, allowing him to push into her, his head falling back as she moved her hips against him, a deep moan falling from her open lips. He reached around and slid his hands under her underwear to grab ahold of her ass, pulling her hips downward to assist in their pleasure. The pulse on the side of his neck quickened as she leaned forward dropping a trail of kisses, her tongue pushing against his pulse before her fangs ripped into him. She pressed her weight down on him, pushing her hips forward as his blood spilled down the back of her throat and quenched one of the fires that burned within, just before she found her additional release. When she felt sated, she stood and took a step back. She adjusted her dress and brushed her hair back from her face. She licked her lips, gathering any remaining blood.

Walking down the aisle to the front of the bus, she tossed one last glance back at the lifeless body slumped over in the seat, his light and hunger extinguished. She smiled as she exited the bus. *He was good . . . good to the last drop.*

She hadn't seen him, but he saw her. *Why the hell would Nika be on a bus?* It certainly didn't suit her lifestyle or her personality. Sebastian had a feeling something was not right. He got out of his car and made a quick call from a phone booth nearby. The machine picked up in Josh's office. He didn't want to leave too much detail in a message, especially since he wasn't sure what was going on. He mentioned seeing Nika and that he was going to follow her. He also mentioned the bus, letting Josh know he had a feeling something was terribly off.

Sebastian ended the call quickly and continued following Nika. She seemed to be on a casual stroll, enjoying the night. This just wasn't her type of neighborhood.

Nika was almost back to the club when she picked up a familiar scent. Funny how she didn't even have to look to know it was him. She entered through the door on the side of the building, nodding to the men just inside. Sebastian entered the club, and the men jumped him, catching him off guard. She watched as they beat the hell out of him until he lost consciousness. The day was turning out better than she thought.

"Move him to one of the platforms on the dance floor and secure his arms to the scaffolding above," Nika ordered. "Then leave the building. Take the rest of the night off."

The men did as she asked, and as Nika ascended the stairs leading up to her office, they heard her say, "I've got a call to make."

The phone was ringing just as Alexis finished getting dressed for her date with Sebastian. "Hello?"

"Alexis, it's Nika."

"It's been a while," Alexis stated dryly.

"Yes, well. That's enough chitchat," Nika retorted in a cool tone. "You need to come to the big club downtown, you know the one. I have a *special* surprise for you."

"What kind of surprise?" she asked, matching Nika's tone.

"The kind only *you* will understand," Nika stated. "Come alone."

The call ended, and Alexis hung up the phone. Her stomach growled, and she knew she needed blood. She walked downstairs to the kitchen and opened the refrigerator. It was filled with containers. The guys really came through for her. They must have stocked it while she was sleeping. She wondered how the conversation with the butcher went. She grabbed a container and downed the contents quickly. *Her new liquid diet. Great.*

She tossed the empty container in the trash and headed for the door. With her new speed, she would be at the club in just a few minutes.

CHAPTER 30

Sebastian was coming to when he noticed Nika circling him like a cat playing with a mouse.

"Wakey wakey," she said with glee.

He moaned, raising his head to look up at her, wincing in pain. He was on his knees with his hands secured at the wrist over his head, and his shirt had been removed. One of his eyes was starting to swell shut, and his bottom lip had been split open in a couple of places, blood trickling from an open wound.

"Oh, poor Sebastian. You are looking a bit worse for wear." Her head fell back, revealing her fangs as she laughed. "Don't worry, your precious Alexis should be here soon."

Sebastian spat blood at her, watching it land on her right cheek. "God, you're even more of a bitch now than you were as a human. I didn't think that was possible. I'll never understand how you and Alexis were best friends."

She wiped his blood from her cheek, licking it off her finger seductively. "Um, well you see, Sebastian, I used to wonder the same thing, and *now* I know it was all a lie." She paced back and forth, studying him. "When I was a measly *human* like you, I wanted nothing more than to be loved and adored like Alexis. Everybody seemed to think she was just the most wonderful person in the world. It was quite irritating. But now," she said, stopping directly in front of him, "I have everything I ever wanted. Power and respect, the kind of respect I deserve."

He managed a chuckle while shaking his head. "Man, becoming a vampire sure didn't increase your intelligence."

"And what is that supposed to mean!" she snapped, taking a step closer to him.

"Confusing fear with respect. It's not the same thing, and if you had half a brain in that head of yours, you would know that."

Nika pulled her right arm back and slapped Sebastian hard across the face. "How dare you speak to me that way!"

Fresh blood poured from the cut in his bottom lip that had almost closed. He turned his head, spitting the blood off to the side, pondering whether he should provoke her any more. She was delusional, but she was still a vampire, and she could kill him anytime she wanted. So why hadn't she. Not that he was in a hurry, but what was she waiting for?

His heart pounded in his chest when he realized Nika was now behind him, whispering in his ear, "Perhaps I won't wait for Alexis." Leaning down, she located his push knife inside his right boot. Removing it, she slowly slid the flat edge of the blade across his hip, continuing until the cool metal contacted his bare skin, leaving a trail from his stomach to his chest.

He remained very still, realizing his only course of action was to remain calm until Alexis arrived. She pressed the blade gently into his right cheek, the tip of it causing a small stinging sensation just before the skin was broken. "Perhaps it's time you learned some respect." She licked his cheek, moaning as she caught the small trace of blood on her tongue.

"Now, now, Miss Nika," Aidan said, walking across the room. "Patience is a virtue."

Nika looked up to see Aidan moving away from the bar, approaching the dance floor. She stood up straight, allowing the blade to fall away from Sebastian's face, still holding it close to his body.

"Sorry, Master. I just thought I would warm him up a bit before she arrived," Nika stated in an apologetic tone.

"I understand, my dear, but we mustn't be hasty. This is something to be savored."

"Aidan," Sebastian managed to say. "I knew there was something I didn't like about you."

"Dear boy," Aidan began, "I would save your strength if I were you." He stopped about five feet from Sebastian. "You are going to need it."

"How about a few nicks here and there?" Nika suggested. "That wouldn't be *all* bad, would it?" A wicked smile crossed her face.

Aidan appreciated her enthusiasm. "No, it wouldn't." He wandered off into the club, knowing their special guest would be arriving soon. He could feel her coming.

Nika grinned, giggling like a schoolgirl as she methodically dragged the edge of the blade across Sebastian's chest and stomach area. He winced in pain, gritting his teeth. The cuts were shallow, like giant papercuts, and they hurt like hell. Blood trickled out slowly as she laughed, sounding like a giddy child playing with a new favorite toy. The smell of his blood and sweat filled the air, causing her natural instincts to pull against her self-control. Her laughter carried across the air, filling the large room like a demented tune.

She leaned down, whispering in his ear. "Don't worry, Sebastian. This will all be over soon. She's here."

Alexis arrived at the club just after the sun disappeared completely from the horizon. She had no idea what was going on with Nika, nor did she have a clue what the surprise would be, but all thoughts led to bad. A sign on the front door stated the club was closed for the next few days due to renovations. No wonder Nika wanted her here. No interruptions.

She walked around the side of the building to the alley and found a door. It was unlocked. She stepped through the doorway, entering a small storage room where there were boxes of supplies stacked along the walls. She moved through the storage area towards another door, pausing for a moment to listen carefully. She heard a female voice in the distance. *Nika.* Pushing the door open, she slowly entered a dimly lit hallway, immediately detecting a familiar scent. Sebastian, and blood. She followed the noise to the main dance floor in the club, noting a staircase on her right. The dance floor was lit up, and she couldn't believe her eyes. There were Nika and Sebastian. He was restrained with his arms tied over his head, and he looked like he had been beaten. There were fresh cuts on his stomach and chest, courtesy of Nika, who held the blade up to her lips, licking it clean.

"Welcome, Alexis," Nika purred. "So, how have you been?"

"Nika, what the hell have you done?" she asked, inching closer to the platform Sebastian was kneeling on. He was in bad shape, real bad shape, and his fresh cuts were tugging at her self-control. "Please stop."

"Oh, sweetie," Nika began, "I wish I could, no wait. I really don't." Again, Nika extended her arm down the length of Sebastian's body, light flashing off the flat of the blade, while the tip sliced through his flesh and left a fresh trail of blood. He grunted in pain, and Alexis watched Nika as she licked the blade clean. "Ooh, Alexis, darling, I certainly can *taste* his appeal, despite how ill-mannered he can be."

Alexis started to move forward, stopping suddenly when she heard a voice. "Alexis, my dear," Aidan said. She turned, watching him approach. "So glad you could join us. We have much to talk about."

"It was *you* who did this to me, wasn't it?" she demanded. "Why?"

Aidan shook his head, his smile fading as he walked around the perimeter of the dance floor. "It actually started many years ago, although, for me, it's like it was just yesterday. Your coven took my sweet Genevieve from me, and I decided to take my revenge." He looked at Alexis. "Let me explain. For many years, my Genevieve and I enjoyed the simple things in life. She was a beauty and a magnificent hunter. Her ruthlessness was beyond compare, and I loved her for it." He paused a moment, amused at the dumbfounded look on her face. "Unfortunately, one night, she came across a young girl who was out for a walk, and she was overcome by the young girl's purity. You see, the girl was special, and she was going to be extremely powerful, which is what made her so irresistible. Genevieve could smell her power, and she just couldn't help herself. She had to have her. What Genevieve didn't know was there was a protection spell cast on the girl by the elders in her coven. Her blood destroyed my Genevieve, and after that, I vowed to destroy your bloodline. Of course, others would benefit from this as well."

"I don't understand," Alexis said. "Why not just kill me? Why turn me into a *monster*?"

Aidan laughed, sneering at the monster reference. Ignoring her question, he continued with his story. "That young girl was your great-aunt. Had she lived, she would have been the most powerful one in the coven, capable of destroying me and my kind." He paused again, walking towards Alexis, pleased when she took a step back. "I was going to kill you. In fact, you should have died in a car accident with your parents *all* those years ago."

Her eyes widened, filled with unshed tears. "Lorcan McCowan," she whispered.

"That's right, my dear," he replied. "You see, when I found out you were still alive, I decided to destroy you another way, and I wanted to do it piece by piece. First, by killing your grandmother, and then finding your best friend in Paris." He looked over at Nika and smiled. His gaze returned to Alexis. "I wanted to do more than just take everything away from you. I wanted to make you feel completely isolated, and I wanted to make sure the bloodline would be irrevocably destroyed. Tainting your blood with mine and *then* changing you was the only way to ensure you wouldn't kill me first. I knew you were protected as well."

"The wine," she stated, shaking her head as all the memories she couldn't recover before now came flooding back into her head.

"Exactly," he whispered, gently running his hand down her cheek. Alexis pulled away, repulsed by his gesture. "Of course, having *all* of you was just an added bonus." Aidan winked at Sebastian from across the room, laughing as Sebastian pulled on his restraints. Alexis looked at Sebastian, at the pain of betrayal on his face.

"See, this way, I get to relish in your pain and misery, *forever*," he said with glee. "Not to mention your friend, who was all *too* eager to help me with my task." He smiled at Nika as she beamed with pride.

"When he found me in Paris," Nika began, slowly walking around to stand in front of Sebastian, "it was like a blessing, to be elevated from my pathetic existence."

Alexis stared at Nika. "I don't understand how you could betray me like this. We were best friends."

"Were we?" Nika asked, moving back and forth in front of Sebastian. "All I remember was how frustrating it was to be friends with somebody who never seemed to do anything wrong according to anybody who met her. *So* loved and adored just for being you. In the meantime, the rest of us had to fight to be taken seriously." Nika rolled her eyes, turning her back on Alexis to walk around Sebastian, who looked like he was barely hanging on. "All I know is how much better things are for me now. I'm happier than I've ever been."

A flash of anger suddenly ripped through Alexis as she bared her teeth and hissed. "Well, I'm not." She took another step forward. "You need to let Sebastian go, Nika."

"I'm afraid that is not going to happen, Alexis," Aidan stated.

She looked back at him. "Why not?"

"My beloved was taken from me, and now it's your turn." He nodded towards Nika.

Alexis turned her head as Nika laughed and leaned down, thrusting the dagger into Sebastian's right kidney. He cried out in pain, and Alexis screamed. She tried to move forward, but she felt a hand on her shoulder attempting to hold her in place. Her training took over, and she spun around, delivering a roundhouse kick to Aidan, sending him flying across the dance floor to the ground. The look on his face was nothing short of astonishment. Alexis turned back towards Nika and Sebastian when she heard Aidan's voice.

"FINISH HIM!"

Nika placed her left hand on top of Sebastian's head, pulling it back as she quickly drew the tip of the blade across the front of his neck. Blood spilled down his chest as his body started twitching, struggling against the trauma inflected on it. Alexis rushed over to him, sliding on her knees across the floor. She pulled her shirt off and pressed it against the front of his throat with her right hand while placing her left hand behind his head to steady it. His hot blood soaked through her shirt, warming her cold hand as she held it in place. The smell of his blood filled the room, pulling at her own bloodlust as her heart and mind were overcome with anguish. She watched his eyes widen, brimming with tears as he gasped for air. A tear fell from his right eye as his gasps came slower, his body no longer pulling against his restraints, until it went slack. She watched the light fade from his eyes, and he was gone.

Alexis couldn't believe what was happening. She stared at Sebastian's lifeless face, his eyes half closed. She reached up, gently closing them completely. Tears fell silently as darkness filled her.

"Now, it's your turn to feel the loss and pain I have experienced for the last sixty years," Aidan said, standing directly behind her. "Come, Nika."

Alexis couldn't take her eyes off Sebastian, but she knew she needed to leave. She didn't want to just leave him, but she didn't have a choice. She needed to find Josh. Why hadn't Sebastian called him before rushing in? WHY? Her head fell back, and she screamed. She loved Sebastian so much. Even as a vampire, she still loved him.

CHAPTER 31

Aidan had won. Her entire world was gone. Alexis looked back up at Sebastian's face a few moments longer, letting her shirt fall away from his neck. His blood flowed slower as it clotted and dried. Her hands were covered. She placed a hand on either side of his face, gently kissing his lips. "I'm so sorry," she whispered.

She needed to go. She needed to find Josh. He was the only one who would be able to help her now. She stood slowly, backing away from the lifeless body. She looked down to see her chest and bra drenched in blood, Sebastian's blood. She needed to clean up, and she needed a shirt. She headed back towards the small storage area. There was a utility sink mounted on the wall where she cleaned herself up as much as possible. She grabbed a jacket hanging on the wall next to the door leading out to the alley. She slipped it on, still struggling with everything that had happened in the last hour. She zipped the jacket up and rolled up the sleeves before leaving the building.

She couldn't believe Nika killed Sebastian and Aidan was really Lorcan McCowan. She felt so betrayed. What did Aidan mean when he said he wouldn't be the only one to benefit from destroying her bloodline? Who was he referring to? She raced to the gym, and she only had to knock once before Josh opened the door.

He could tell from the look on her face something was terribly wrong. He stepped back so she could enter the gym, and as soon as the door closed, they shared an embrace.

"I can't believe this is happening," Alexis managed to say. There should have been tears, but she didn't seem to have any more at the moment.

"I know," was all Josh could say.

"How *did* you know?" Alexis asked, pulling back to look at him.

"Sebastian left a message on my machine, saying he was following Nika. Then a buddy from my unit called me," he began, his gaze looking down at first. "Some people saw a bus sitting underneath an overpass. It had been sitting there for some time. The police were called, and the driver was found dead, strange marks on his neck, and he was also in a partial state of undress. A witness said he saw a young woman around the time the bus stopped. A redhead."

"Nika," she stated.

"Yes," he replied. "Sebastian must have seen her and decided to follow her." He looked across the gym with a distant stare before walking towards his office. Alexis followed. He took a seat in his office chair, and she sat across from him. They sat in silence for a moment.

"Nika is not the only concern we have," she stated.

"What do you mean?" he asked.

"Turns out, Sebastian was right about Aidan. He is Lorcan McCowan," she said, "the one who killed my entire family."

"Why?" he asked.

"Because of Genevieve," she stated, staring at him. "She was the love of his life. Genevieve killed my great-aunt, but what she didn't know was my great-aunt had a protection spell put on her by the coven. Her blood killed Genevieve."

Josh stared at Alexis in disbelief, trying to wrap his mind around everything. "How many years has this guy been holding a grudge?"

"From what he described, at least sixty," she stated, finding it difficult to believe, herself. "Aidan found Nika in Paris. He manipulated her, turned her into a vampire, and used her to destroy me and everything I care about. I had no idea she really hated me. She's sadistic. She killed Sebastian right in from of me." Alexis paused, looking down at the ground, a single tear falling from her eye. "I had no idea she could be *so* cruel."

Josh bowed his head. "I'm so sorry, Alexis. I failed."

"What do you mean?" She stared at him, confused by his statement.

"I wasn't there for my best friend, and I have to live with that the rest of my life," he declared, looking into her eyes, his usually stoic face filled with emotion.

She stood up and walked around the desk, kneeling beside him. She reached out, placing her right hand it on his leg. "It wasn't your fault, and I certainly don't blame you. I blame Nika and Aidan for . . ." Alexis paused, rage filling her. She stood, slowly backing away from Josh, keeping her head low. She could feel herself shifting as everything became more acute. She could hear Josh's heartbeat calling her, tickling her senses, his scent washing over her. A pang of hunger pulled from the depths of her.

"What's the matter?" he asked, and then he heard it. "Did you just growl?"

"Stay still!" Panic filled her voice. "Stay where you are!" She continued backing up until she felt the wall behind her.

"Alexis?" Josh shifted in his chair, trying to make eye contact with her. "Alexis look at me."

She lifted her head, looking deep into his eyes, growling again and baring her teeth like a wild animal before it attacked.

"Are you okay?" he asked.

"I . . . I don't know," she managed to say. "Suddenly all I want to do is devour you."

"Oddly, that has an entirely different meaning than the first time I ever imagined you saying that to me," he said, trying to lighten the mood. He *was* nervous though. "Sorry. What can I do?"

"Be very still. I just need to calm down." She closed her eyes, focusing on calming her mind. She could feel her hunger and frustration growing, and she sensed Josh was becoming more concerned. She looked at him, trying not to fixate on the pulse in his neck. The strength of his scent faded as she found her control. He was the last link to who she was, and it would be a shame if she hurt him.

"I'm okay now," she finally said. "I was really concerned I was going to kill you for a minute."

"*You* were concerned?" he asked with a chuckle.

"I'm sorry, Josh. You are the last person I want to hurt right now. Nika, on the other hand. I think it would bring me *great* pleasure to destroy her. I'm not sure what to do about Aidan, though. He's so strong."

"Maybe I can help you with Nika," he stated.

"I can't ask you to do that. I won't put you in the line of fire."

"I won't be in the line of fire. I'm actually the perfect one to get close to her and take her out." He paused for a moment, deep in thought.

"What?" She knew whatever idea just popped into his head would be intriguing and crazy.

"She's never met me. She will have no idea who I am. I'll go to the club and offer my services as a personal bodyguard," he explained. "I'll create a need for her to want to hire a personal bodyguard."

"And just how do you plan on doing that?"

"I've got somebody who owes me a favor. He deals in special weapons, both obtaining and making. I know he'll have something or know how to make something that can do the job right."

"Okay, but why would she want to hire you?" she asked.

"Because I'm going to initiate a situation that will make her feel needy and perhaps a bit vulnerable."

"Well, it's gotta be *some* situation. I know since *I* became a vampire, not much makes me nervous anymore."

"It will take some creative thinking," Josh stated. "Give me a couple of days."

"Okay, then, all we have to worry about is Aidan. Once we take Nika out, he's going to come after us and, no offense, Josh, but I don't think all your training is going to make that much of a difference. As it is, I don't even know if *I* could protect you from him."

"I'm aware of the dangers. I'm crazy, but I'm not stupid." Suddenly his expression changed, and Alexis knew he was having another crazy thought.

"What?" She hesitated. "Josh?"

"There is one thing you could do that would give me more of an edge, make me better than I am now. It would certainly make me stronger."

"What's that?" she asked, studying his face.

"Turn me. Make me like you."

Alexis couldn't believe what she was hearing. Shaking her head, she turned away from Josh and walked out of his office. He waited for a moment before going after her. She was standing by the sparring ring, her back to him when she began to speak.

"You're insane." Her voice was low. She turned to face him, her eyes filled with distress. "Why would you ask me to do such a thing?"

He took a step closer, and she took a step back.

"Alexis," he began, "let me explain."

"All right," she responded. "Explain. Explain to me why the hell you want me to turn you into a monster."

"After you were turned, Sebastian and I talked about what to do if anything ever happened to him. Alexis, he knew how I felt about you, how I *really* felt about you. He also knew I respected him and our friendship too much to ever act on my feelings." He paused for a moment, gathering his thoughts. "I don't want you to be alone, Alexis, and neither did Sebastian. You need somebody on your side who knows and understands what you need now. Somebody you can trust, somebody who cares about you."

She was moved by his words but still bothered by his request. "I'm sorry, Josh. I care about you too, but the thought of destroying you . . ." She dropped her eyes, unable to finish her sentence.

"Have you ever wondered why I've never talked about my family? It's because I don't have any family, especially now that Sebastian is gone. He was like a brother to me. He *was* my family. He showed me what having a close family was all about. Alexis, I've always had a dark soul, it's why I fight the way I do. Part of me really enjoys causing pain. Sebastian was the one who helped me find more balance." He paused a moment. "I understand what you're saying, and I appreciate the fact that you're trying to save what's left of my humanity, my soul, but we *are* at war here. We need every advantage we can get." He reached out, taking her hands in his, and she looked up into his eyes. "Alexis, just promise me if things get bad, you will consider it."

She hesitated for a moment, studying his face. "I promise if there is no other way, I will consider it, but then I'm no better than Aidan."

"Yes, you are, because I'm asking you to do it. You weren't given an option."

Alexis pulled away, moving further across the mats. She needed some distance.

Josh watched her for a second. He could tell her thoughts were somewhere else. "What are you thinking about now?"

"Sebastian's family," she stated quietly. "They have no idea what's happened." She turned to face him, unshed tears in her eyes. "How am I going to tell them?"

"You're not," he stated. "I will take care of it." He watched as her head fell back, fresh tears rolling down her cheeks. "Alexis, this was not your fault."

She wiped her tears away. "Thank you, Josh. I know how much this is affecting you right now, and I've known how you've *always* felt about me."

"So my confession was for nothing?" he joked.

"No, not for nothing." She managed a smile. She appreciated his honesty, not that he really had a choice. She could smell his desire for her, along with every other emotion he was feeling. Becoming a vampire had somehow heightened her empathic abilities, or perhaps it was simply because she was a predator now.

"Give me a few days to put a little concern into Nika's existence," he said. "I'll go see my friend and tell him what I need to take care of her."

She nodded, but he could tell she was thinking about something else now.

"While you're dealing with Nika, I need to go deal with another individual who has betrayed me."

He cocked his head to one side. “Dare I ask?”

“It seems like every time I need some personal business handled or I want to make a change to my assets, something gets in the way. Mr. Blake is the only one who knows about all my holdings, the ones Gram set up for me. I think he is slipping information to Aidan, but I need proof.”

“Are you serious? What are you going to do?”

“If it is true, and Blake is the one leaking the information to Aidan, then Mr. Blake may learn Aidan Drake is not the only force to be reckoned with,” she announced with a smile. “It might be time to introduce Mr. Blake to the real me.”

He couldn’t help but laugh. “That poor bastard has no idea what’s coming.”

“No, he doesn’t,” she said in a cool tone.

CHAPTER 32

Sebastian's family was devastated. It had been a few days since Josh had broken the news to them, but they didn't blame Alexis, according to Josh. There was concern about the rest of the family's well-being though, which was understandable.

Alexis called their house several times a few weeks after the news, only to get the answering machine. The last call she made was answered by an automated voice telling her the number was no longer in service. She grabbed her leather jacket and raced out of the house.

Alexis reached the Kincaid house just after dusk, to see a few lights on in the living room through the window and the trunk open on their car in the driveway. She approached the front door slowly, stopping dead in her tracks when it opened. Claire, Dennis, and Maxi were coming out of the house with luggage, and they stopped just outside the door when they saw her, fear and hesitation on their faces.

"You're leaving?" Alexis asked. "Why?"

"With everything that has happened . . ." Claire paused, lowering her head as her eyes filled with tears. "You understand how difficult it is for us to stay here now that we've lost Sebastian, don't you?"

Alexis wanted to move closer to them, but the smell of their fear made her stop. The last thing she wanted was for them to fear her. "Yes, I understand. I understand better than anyone," she said. "But how can you leave? You were there for me after Gram was killed, and now that I've lost Sebastian . . ."

"I'm sorry, Alexis," Claire said. "If there were any other way, but the coven doesn't want anybody else tainted or lost. Lorcan has stolen *so* much from all of us already, and after what he did to you, the coven just can't risk losing anybody else."

Part of Alexis understood what Claire was saying, and the other part didn't give a damn. "So I'm being punished for something that wasn't even my choice?" She glanced at Claire and Dennis, before her eyes fell to Maxi. She could feel the young girl's pain. She had lost her big brother, and she didn't have a choice either. She was still under her parents' guardianship, being a minor. She had to leave. "Maxi," she began. Maxi started moving forward, but Dennis put his hand on her shoulder. "Maxi, stay strong," Alexis said.

Maxi nodded, tears rolling silently down her cheeks. She and Alexis had become so close in the last few months. Alexis was like a sister to her. "You too," she managed to say. "I'm going to miss you."

The three of them began walking down the sidewalk towards the car. Alexis stepped back, out of respect. Dennis finished loading the rest of the suitcases in the trunk, and when he slammed the trunk Alexis flinched. She watched as they got into the car and drove away. She was pissed. Rage and sorrow filled her, and she needed to get rid of all the negative energy. She took off running and didn't stop until she reached the water.

Looking out over the water always calmed her down. The sound of the waves crashing against the pillars and the underside of the pier soothed her racing thoughts. She had been spending a lot of time down by the pier late at night. It was the best time for her to be out with the lowest risk of running into a lot of people, and tonight was no different. She closed her eyes, pushing her pain out across the water, feeling calmer each time the cool mist sprayed back on her face, then she smelled his approach.

"Hey, baby," a gruff voice said. "How's about you and me havin' a little fun?"

Alexis turned to see a hulk of a man standing near her. Emptiness filled his eyes, the smile on his face nothing short of lecherous. She smirked. "Sorry, this baby is not in the mood."

"That's all right," he replied. "I can change that." He pulled a knife out of his back pocket, his thumb pushing against the flipper to display an oversized curved blade glistening under the nearly full moon.

Her eyes lingered on the blade, and she laughed out loud. "Oh, honey, you just did." Before the hulk knew what was happening, Alexis was behind him. She drove the blade deep into his back, sinking her teeth into the side of his neck. Any noise was muffled by her hand pressed tightly over his mouth. When she was done, she pushed his body into the water, feeling much calmer and satisfied.

CHAPTER 33

Alexis needed to leave Seattle. Since everybody she cared about was either dead or had left town, there was nothing left for her here, except Josh, but who knew for how long. It depended on how his plan to get rid of Nika went and Aidan's reaction. Alexis knew Aidan would be angry, and she knew she just might have to turn Josh to save him. If nothing else, both would have to disappear.

The weapon was done, and Josh had stopped by late last week to show it to her. It was exquisite, and she knew Nika would love it. Josh's plan was already in place, and Nika had put out word she wanted more personal security around her.

In the meantime, Alexis had verified where the interference was coming from with her financial holdings. She needed to do something about it soon, but she needed to make sure nothing would stand in her way.

Josh arrived at the club around four thirty Saturday afternoon. He noticed a guy already at the front door despite the fact that it was hours before the club opened. *Interesting.* The guy opened the door to speak with Josh.

"Can I help you?" he asked.

"Yes," Josh replied. "I have an appointment with Nika this afternoon. My name is Josh."

"More like an audition," the guy smirked.

Josh understood the guy's meaning, but it didn't really matter. He was already on full alert. He stepped through the doorway, pausing for a moment before glancing back at the doorman, who was sizing him up. He understood why. At six foot four and 210 pounds, people didn't always understand why his nickname was Reaper. For those who really wanted to know, he would happily show them.

"Go down the hall to the main dance floor and wait," the guy directed.

Josh nodded, acknowledging the order. Walking down the hall, he picked up the scents of cleaning products and the residuals of sweat and cigarettes. There was a stairwell off to the right, probably where her office was located. He would get the full tour in a few minutes.

The hall wrapped around a corner to the left, leading straight out onto the main dance floor. He paused for a moment at the edge of the room, noticing the bar to the left, with seating that wrapped all the way around the room. There were also a few smaller dance platforms off to the side of the main floor. He remembered Alexis telling him how Sebastian was killed and where. These had to be the platforms she was talking about. He wondered how often they were used. Guess he would find out soon enough.

"Come to the center of the floor," a female voice said. It was more of a demand than a request.

He stepped out onto the dance floor and noticed a man standing on the other side. He was maybe around five nine, and he had some size to him, well, girth anyway, not that it really mattered.

"Stop there," the voice said.

Josh stopped in the middle of the floor, staring at the man for a moment before glancing up to the balcony. Alexis had shown him a picture of Nika. There she was, sitting as if she were the queen of the Colosseum. He laughed internally. It reminded him of Roman times. He noticed another man standing next to her, who seemed different from the one staring him down from across the floor.

"Turn around for me and remove your shirt."

Josh turned around, removing his shirt at the same time. He tossed it off to the side, looking back at the guy standing at the opposite edge of the dance floor. The guy smirked, and Josh knew he had him. It was one thing when people thought the biggest guy in the room was the toughest. It was quite another when the biggest guy in the room also held that misconception. *Guess it's time for a lesson.*

"So, Josh," Nika began, "I am looking for a reason why I should hire *you* and send Little Mickey here on his way." Her tone was mocking and not lost on the man standing across from him.

The man quickly looked up at the balcony, his expression now angry, unaware Nika wanted him gone.

"But Miss Nika," Mick started, moving onto the dance floor, "I've apologized several times for the mistake."

"The *mistake*?" Nika retorted, glaring at Mick. "You mean *your* mistake." She cast her eyes to Josh. "So, Josh, let's see what you've got."

Mick moved further across the dance floor, lumbering straight for Josh, his emotions driving the attack, always a big mistake. Rushing forward, he swung at Josh's head with a right hook, which Josh easily outmaneuvered. Josh ducked low and pivoted on his right foot, catching Mick in the gut with a reverse left side kick. Mick doubled over as Josh stepped to the side, waiting for him to recover. Once upright, Mick turned towards Josh, his face red with frustration. He approached Josh again, a little slower this time, but Josh was ready when Mick came in with a combination of jabs and a cross, all easily blocked by Josh using "sticky hands." The more frustrated Mick became, the more difficult Josh found it not to laugh. *This* guy was a bodyguard? No wonder Nika wanted him gone.

"STOP!" Nika called down. "This is boring. *Show* me why I should hire you."

Josh was still looking up at Nika when Mick came at him again from the side. Josh reacted quickly, catching Mick in the front of the throat with his left elbow, leaving him gasping for air, followed by his left foot coming up and then down at an angle against Mick's right leg just below the knee, breaking both the tibia and the fibula simultaneously. The cracking of bones echoed throughout the room as Mick landed in a heap on the floor, one hand on his throat and the other on his leg. Josh knew the man would never be the same when he saw the bones had torn through the fabric of his pants.

Nika beamed with delight. "Excellent!" She applauded with enthusiasm. "Now, somebody please clean up this mess before our guests arrive." A few men appeared from the bar area to move Mick off the dance floor. "Adam," she said, turning to the man beside her, "would you please show Mr. Josh upstairs to my office?"

He nodded and watched Josh retrieve his shirt, pulling it on over his head. Josh walked off the dance floor, not bothering to look at the man he put down. Heading back down the hall towards the stairs he had passed earlier, Josh caught a glance from the bouncer who had let him in the door. The bouncer gave him a nod, his demeanor the opposite of what it was before. Josh reached the stairs and was greeted by the man from the balcony.

"My name is Adam," the man said, extending his right hand.

Josh shook his hand, sizing him up. The guy was in great shape and nothing like the embarrassment he just dealt with.

"Welcome aboard. Follow me, please."

Josh followed Adam up the stairs and down a long hallway, passing an opening on the left which led to the balcony where Nika had been sitting. At the end of the hall, they stopped in front of a door. Adam knocked once. They entered the office, and Josh looked around, taking in the décor. It didn't really look like an office, but he wasn't sure what he would call it. There was a vanity in the corner across from the door they came through. In the center of the room was a library table behind a large sofa, facing an oversized desk in the far corner of the room next to a wet bar. All the furniture looked rather oversized and ornate. Too much for the room, like Nika herself.

"Well, here you are," Nika purred, stepping out from behind her desk. Josh studied her as she moved towards him wearing a royal-blue jumpsuit with a plunging neckline, her eyes looking him over from head to toe. She stopped about three feet from him, her sweet smile a drastic contrast to what he knew her true nature to be. "Josh, is it?" she asked. He nodded. "I noticed a tattoo just above your right shoulder blade, a figure holding a weapon. What does the tattoo represent?"

"A nickname I acquired several years ago."

"And what nickname was that?" She cocked her head to one side, studying his face.

"Reaper. The weapon is a scythe."

She smiled, stepping forward. She placed her right hand in the center of his chest. "Aptly chosen," she purred. She looked him deep in the eyes for a moment before turning away. "That was wonderful work you performed on Mick." She walked towards the bar and poured a glass of champagne. "Is that the level of service I should expect from you when protecting me?" She looked at him again.

"If that's what is required."

Nika tipped her glass, emptying its contents. "Excellent," she replied, grinning from ear to ear. "You can go now. Be back here tonight at eight p.m."

"As you wish." He moved towards the door.

"Oh, and, Reaper," Nika called.

Josh turned his head as he reached the door.

"Welcome aboard."

Josh smiled and nodded. Opening the door, he heard her voice again.

"Come to me, Adam. I have some *energy* to burn off."

Josh stepped through the doorway, catching the reflection in the vanity mirror of Adam lifting Nika up on top of the desk. He leaned in to kiss her as Josh pulled the door shut. *Good to know.* Josh might have to readjust Adam's loyalties later if he could.

CHAPTER 34

It was a good night for a walk, but this walk had a purpose. Alexis had finally put all the pieces together and figured out Mr. Blake *had* betrayed her, and she was pissed. The rain was coming down in sheets as she waited just around the corner. She adjusted the hood on her jacket, standing in the darkness of the alley between the law offices and the parking garage. It was the perfect place to wait, to catch him before he got to his car. The rainstorm was not unusual for this time of year, but the thunder seemed to be a bonus. It could come in handy if things got louder than expected.

She had thought about confronting him in his office, but that would lead to many questions and unwanted attention. Besides, she already had all the proof she needed. She had managed to get into Mr. Blake's office and pull her files. Notes from conversations with Aidan revealed everything. Making Alexis a vampire was not enough. He wanted to keep her around to torture her on other levels. *What a bastard.* No, this would be much better.

Alexis smiled at the thought of Mr. Blake suffering. What he had done was inexcusable, betraying her like he did. *What the hell ever happened to lawyer-client confidentiality?* Besides, she was hungry. She'd been surviving mostly off blood in containers, so the prospect of a hot meal was exciting.

The wind shifted, and she picked up his scent, and that damn cologne, of which he wore too much. She smiled to herself thinking about all the problems she was going to resolve taking care of this one individual who obviously had no respect for anyone else.

Mr. Blake moved quickly between the two structures, when something grabbed him and threw him up against the side of the building in the alley. The force of contact with the structure knocked the wind out of him, causing him to double over. Regaining his composure, he didn't have to look far to see who had done this to him.

"Good evening, Mr. Blake," Alexis purred, a wicked smile across her face.

"Miss McBain," he said, surprised. "What are you doing here?"

"Well, I'm waiting for you, of course." She walked slowly towards him.

"Perhaps this can wait," he stammered, looking around. "I'm late for a meeting with a client, and he prefers it when I'm prompt."

"Mm, I'm sure he does," she said, inching closer to him, her eyes holding his gaze. "It seems we have a *mutual* acquaintance of sorts."

Blake looked confused and nervous at the same time. "Oh yeah? Who might that be?" He looked around to see if anybody could help him. Something was different about her; he just didn't know what.

"Oh, come now," she began. "You know who I mean."

"Um, no?"

He didn't have to say the name out loud because Alexis could already taste the man's fear on her tongue, and it was *delicious*.

"I am talking about Aidan Drake." She was close enough to feel the pounding in his heart dancing across her skin, standing out from the rain cascading down around them. It was intoxicating. She felt herself shift, her fangs dripping with excitement.

"Please . . . you don't want to kill me," Blake said nervously.

"Why the hell not?" she said, smiling, eyes fixed on him. "I know now you were the one keeping tabs on me, sharing information with Mr. Drake." She pushed her hood back off her head, the contrast of her dark soaked hair against her pale skin. She was delighted to see more fear in his eyes.

"What are you?" His voice was shaky.

"What am I?" Stepping forward, she reached up to caress the front lapel of his coat. "I am what Aidan Drake made me. I am the last thing you will see."

"Please, I'm *so* sorry," he pleaded. "You have no idea how persuasive Mr. Drake can be."

"Actually, I do, or did you miss something during our conversation?" Her lips parted. "Besides, one less lawyer in the world won't be a bad thing."

Alexis leaned forward, pulling Blake towards her. As her fangs found the pulse in the side of his neck, his screams were lost under the loud crackle of thunder. She drained him, enjoying the freedom she felt in killing him.

She released his lapel and watched his body slide down the side of the building, landing in a heap on the ground. She pulled her hood back up over her head, turning to walk away when she realized it was times like this Alexis had finally come to terms with what she had become.

CHAPTER 35

Nika felt even more beautiful as a vampire than she did when she was human. Sitting in front of the mirror of her vanity table, she admired her reflection as she got ready for another evening at the club. The remodel had gone well, and everybody was enjoying the new atmosphere she had created. The club was now the hottest place to be in the city, thanks to her.

She thought about Adam while she brushed her hair. He was quite spectacular, for a human. She thought about turning him, but she enjoyed having the upper hand.

Nika smiled, thinking about how different her existence was now, although some things never changed. She still loved shopping and flirting. The ability to go into any store and purchase whatever she wanted was nothing new to her, coming from a wealthy family. However, if a silly shop girl became an irritation, she would just kill her, something Aidan was not happy about, having to remind her to be discreet. But sometimes she couldn't help herself. *How else were they going to learn?*

She paused for a moment, glancing around *her* office. She had completely redone the space in some of her favorite periods, rococo and baroque. She had brought in a decorator, and everything had been redesigned from the flooring to the paint on the walls. Gorgeous heavy drapes covered the windows, royal purple with accents of gold, which brought out the ornate moldings she had added to the walls all around the room. At first, she was concerned the colors would be too much for Aidan's taste, then she remembered he had been around during that era.

She was finishing her hair when she heard a knock on her door and Josh appeared in the room from nowhere.

"Where's Adam?" she asked.

"He had to run an errand, but he should be back soon," he replied, walking across the room to answer the door.

Josh had sent Adam away, permanently. Having Adam around would have made it more difficult to take care of Nika, and Josh had been working at the club long enough to see the struggle Adam was having with his emotions towards her. He also confided in Josh, telling him Nika was not what she appeared to be, showing him the bite marks on the inside of his wrists. Josh told Adam he knew and advised him to leave town immediately. Adam didn't argue, which was good. He was just another victim of Nika's, and after tonight, her last. Josh had discovered an incinerator in the basement, something he figured would come in handy.

Nika was still fixated on her hair when Josh appeared with a brown box. She paused, watching him walk over to the library table to set it down. Her emerald-green eyes filled with excitement.

"What is that?" she asked, jumping up.

"Wait, Ms. LaRue," Josh urged.

"What?"

"Adam told me about the last time a mysterious box showed up for you, and to be honest, I don't really want to be fired like Mick."

Josh had sent a mysterious gift to the club a few weeks ago, shortly after Nika had killed Sebastian. When the contents were removed from the box, a mechanism sprayed holy water across the front of Nika's dress, also contacting her skin. Screams filled the office as her skin melted before her eyes. According to Adam, Nika spent the rest of the evening in her office, inviting guests upstairs to meet her, who were never seen again.

"Oh, how stupid of me. Please, open the box."

She backed away from the table, allowing Josh to step forward. Lifting the top off slowly, he set it off to the side. A crisp white envelope with "Ms. Nika LaRue" written on the front was lying inside the box.

"There is an envelope addressed to you," he stated. "Would you like me to open it?"

"Yes."

Josh opened the envelope carefully, as Nika's impatience grew. He pulled a card out of the envelope and glanced over the writing. "It's from a Mr. Drake." He handed the card to her.

Nika took it and read.

Miss Nika,

Thank you again, my dear, for adding such beauty to my establishment. Please accept this as a small token of my appreciation.

Aidan Drake

Nika smiled, holding the card tightly to her chest. She watched Josh remove a long, sapphire-blue jewelry box, trimmed in gold piping. She took a step closer, her eyes fixed on the box, and Josh took a step back, allowing her to get even closer. Slowly, she opened the box, gasping when she saw the necklace inside resting on blue satin. She stared for a moment, carefully taking in every detail of the incredible gift before her. She had seen a lot of beautiful things in her life, but she had never seen anything like this. A Tahitian pearl, the largest she had ever seen, set in titanium. On either side towards the top of the chain were four diamonds, graduating in size from half a carat to one and a half carats, flawless in color and clarity. Lifting her left hand, she gently caressed the side of the necklace, mesmerized for a moment with a smile on her face.

"Miss LaRue, are you all right?"

"Yes," she mumbled softly.

"Would you like to wear it tonight?"

"Absolutely." She smiled to herself. Aidan must really be happy with the remodel she had done to the club. She wanted to please him, which was unlike her because she'd never cared about pleasing anybody before she met him.

Josh carefully removed the necklace from the box, unclasping the sides. He turned to look at Nika, a sparkle in her eyes and a smile across her face. She turned, pulling her hair off to the left as his arms reached over her head. He paused, allowing the huge pearl to dangle for a second in front of her face. She sighed as he encircled her neck with the necklace, her fiery locks spilling down across her left shoulder. *What an incredible gift!* She reached up to caress the necklace again when she felt metal touch her throat, followed by a sharp pain when something pierced her flesh. She tried to pull the necklace away as her own blood soaked the front of her dress, suddenly realizing there was a metal hook embedded in the front of her throat. Then she heard his voice.

"This is for killing my best friend," Josh whispered. He pressed down on the top two diamonds, separating them from the lower ones and allowing a wire to unspool from inside the center of the large pearl. He crossed the two ends of the necklace behind her neck, and the wire cut through her flesh with ease. He watched her head roll off the top of her shoulders and her body crumble to the floor.

It was done, and now he had to move fast. He needed to get rid of the body, burn it, and get out of the club before she was expected to make an appearance. He dropped the necklace on the floor next to her before walking over to the window and pulling one of the heavy drapes down. He spread it over the top of the body, tucking the edge of the fabric underneath. Then he pulled the second window drape down, spreading it out at the edge of the body. He rolled the body up in the drapery until it was completely covered, noting the heavy fabric conveniently absorbing any blood.

He stood up, looking around the room. *Shit! The head!* It had rolled across the room towards the vanity area, leaving a blood trail. He smiled and walked over to retrieve it. *A special little gift for Aidan, the bastard.* Grabbing a handful of red hair, he placed the head on top of the vanity, right in the center so it would be the first thing anybody saw when they entered the room. Josh smiled, realizing he *may* be enjoying this a little too much. *Screw it!*

He walked back over to the rolled-up body and picked it up, throwing it over his right shoulder before heading for the door. He slowly opened the door, looking to the left, then the right. Stepping out of the room, he closed the door behind him when Victoria, a co-worker, came walking down the hall from the balcony area, looking a little too curious for his comfort.

"What's going on?" she asked.

"Ms. Nika suddenly decided the drapes in her room just had to go, so she demanded I take them down and burn them. You know how she can be."

"Okay, well, I just came up to let her know her table is ready, and Mr. Drake will be arriving within a half hour." Victoria started to take a step closer to the door as Josh blocked her path. She stared at him, an inquisitive look on her face.

"I will let Ms. Nika know after I run this down to the incinerator. You go back and double-check to make sure everything is perfect. The mood she is in, trust me when I say we don't want to make her unhappy."

"Are you sure?" she asked.

"Oh yeah. I've got this," he replied with a smile.

"Okay." Victoria pivoted, walking back down the hall and stepping back onto the balcony where Nika's special table was located. Victoria knew Nika loved sitting in the balcony because it allowed her to look out over the entire club, like a queen looking down on her subjects.

That was close. Josh turned, quickly walking the short distance in the opposite direction, across the hall to go down to the basement. Just as he reached the bottom of the stairs, he heard a scream. *Damn girl! She never could take direction very well.* He crossed the room to the incinerator in just a few steps, opening the doors and tossing the body inside before pushing the button to ignite the flames. He closed the doors securely, racing to the back door leading out to the alley. Just as he opened it, he heard all the different voices full of anger and excitement.

"He's killed her! Find him! Find him NOW!" a deep male voice called out.

Shit! Time to go! He ran down the back alley, expertly climbing over the fence before disappearing into the night. He needed to get out of there and meet Alexis back at the gym to let her know it was done.

CHAPTER 36

Josh traveled down as many back alleys leading to the gym as he could, carefully avoiding the main streets to stay out of sight. Rounding the last corner, he reached the door of his gym, casting a final glance over his shoulder before putting the key in the lock. Movement out of the corner of his eye caused him to spin around ready to attack until he realized it was Alexis.

"Damn!" he exclaimed.

"Sorry, I didn't mean to startle you." She studied him for a moment, surprised by his reaction. She also detected a level of concern from him, one she'd never seen before.

"Well, it's done," he said. "Let's get inside."

Josh unlocked the door, and Alexis followed him in. Locking the door, he made his way quickly back towards his office with Alexis right behind him. She could tell something was up.

There wasn't anybody at the gym, and there wouldn't be for a while. Josh had already let all his regulars know the gym would be closed temporarily with no reopening date scheduled. He told Dave, his assistant manager, to take the next few weeks off with pay while he figured out what he was going to do. Dave had served in the military with him, so Josh knew he could be trusted to handle things while he was out of town. Dave appreciated the paid time off, and Josh told him he would be in touch soon.

"So . . . I take it there was a problem?"

"Well," he started to explain.

She stared at him, waiting.

"When I was moving the body down to the incinerator, I ran into an employee coming to the office to tell Nika her table was ready. She saw the rolled-up drapes over my shoulder, so I told her Nika wanted the drapes gone. I told her *I* would let Nika know her table was ready, and then I sent her away."

"What happened?"

"As soon as I got down to the basement, I heard a scream, so I knew she decided to go into Nika's office."

Alexis looked at him, perplexed. "You cleaned up, so what made her scream?"

Josh dropped his gaze for a second, but he couldn't hide the smile as it swept across his face, and Alexis didn't miss his pulse speed up with excitement.

"Josh! What did you do?"

Josh glanced around the room before speaking. "I sort of propped the head up on top of the vanity, facing the door so it would be the first thing somebody saw when they entered the room."

"Oh, shit!" she exclaimed. "Why?"

"Because I wanted to send Aidan a message," he announced proudly.

"Was that message 'Come get me'?" she asked in a mocking tone.

"Alexis, I know being vindictive doesn't come by you naturally, but look at everything you have been through in the last few months. Nika got what she deserved, and Aidan will too."

Alexis turned, taking a few steps away from him before she started laughing, causing Josh to become nervous. He glanced towards the door, wondering if he should put some distance between the two of them. She turned to face him, his fear dancing across her skin appealed to her darkness. Her smile only increased his concern.

"It's okay, Josh. I'm not going to hurt you."

"You're not?"

"No. I understand why you did what you did." She paused. "I seem to be developing a darker sense of humor these days. It was funny."

"You really think so?" he asked with some hesitation.

"I do. I'm okay."

"That's good to know because I wasn't trying to make you mad."

"I know," she said. "The problem is, Aidan will be furious, and I don't think I can protect you."

"You may not be able to protect me, but I can."

"You don't mean . . ." she began.

"Yes, I do," he said, walking over to her. "Turn me, Alexis."

She shook her head. She couldn't believe what she was hearing. "I can't."

"It's the only way to ensure my safety. You *have* to change me now."

"There has to be another way," she said, pacing in front of him. She couldn't believe he was still asking her to turn him. She stopped, locking eyes with him. "You have no idea what's in store for you if I do this."

"Yes, I do. Look, I know I'm damn good at what I do, but you were right. Even with all my skills, there is no way in hell I can beat a vampire."

Alexis turned away from him, walking over to the chair in front of the desk. She sat sideways, staring at the floor. Josh walked over and knelt in front of her. She sat back in the chair, surprised they were eye to eye. She stared into his eyes, thinking about everything she had lost. She would never love him like she'd loved Sebastian, but she didn't want anything to happen to him either. They did have a bond, and she trusted him, completely.

"Josh," she began, "I care about you, but I've already lost *so* much. The thought of destroying you . . ."

"You won't be destroying me. And you certainly won't be losing me. You will be creating an ally."

She chuckled. "Way to put a positive spin on it."

Josh reached out with his left hand, caressing her face, her skin cold to the touch. She was still the most beautiful woman he had ever seen and the strongest woman he had ever known. "Alexis, I know we just lost Sebastian, and I would never want to disrespect his memory or what you two had."

"I know, Josh."

"I loved Sebastian like a brother. He *was* my family." He paused, staring into her eyes for a moment. "You also know how I feel about you."

"I do."

He pulled his hand back, dropping his gaze.

"Josh, I know how much you want me." She stared at him for a moment. "So much has happened, and at times I can't believe this is my existence, but I also know whatever happens now will never betray what Sebastian and I once had. I'm different now, and so are my views on many things." She gently reached up, brushing her fingertips across his bottom lip. “I can only think of one way to change you and make it less painful, but it would just be for tonight.”

“I know,” he replied, smiling. “Although, I am surprised you’re offering.”

Alexis smiled. “What can I say, a girl’s gotta eat.” She leaned forward, and he met her halfway, his lips hot against hers. She craved his warmth. The truth was, she craved human touch. She reached forward, pulling his hips between her legs, her hands sliding under his shirt, caressing his sides. His skin was hot and smooth, his energy tickling her fingertips. He held her face between his hands as their kiss deepened. Alexis felt the shift, her senses more acute as his desire for her filled the room, intoxicating her.

He pulled back, staring into her eyes again. “Alexis, I have nothing else for me here.”

She nodded, understanding exactly what he meant.

He stood, pulling her up at the same time. He reached for her hand and walked backward, and she followed him into the small room behind the office. He kissed her harder as they pulled at each other’s clothes, tossing them on the floor. Alexis sat down on the bed, lying back and gazing up at Josh with hungry eyes. He leaned down and crawled up her naked body, the warmth of him burning her skin with the promise of release. He bit her neck passionately, and she cried out as he entered her. They both moaned with pleasure as their bodies fused together in a passionate dance. His body was strong and had everything she needed. They moved as one, and she could feel his heart beating faster and faster, his blood calling to her. His breath blew hot against her shoulder, and when his body started to tense, she ran her tongue along his neck and found the strong pulse waiting for her. Placing a hand on the back of his head, she pulled him down towards her hungry mouth, and as her razor-sharp fangs pierced his skin, she heard a sharp inhale from him as his blood flowed down the back of her throat, causing her to shudder with pleasure, drowning in metallic euphoria.

His movements started to slow as she drank him in, a soft sigh escaping his lips. The full weight of his body melted into hers as his pulse slowed. Rolling him over onto his back, she straddled him.

"Josh, can you hear me?" she whispered. His eyes fluttered a bit. Alexis bit her wrist, holding it over his parted lips. "Drink."

She pressed her wrist against his mouth, feeling his hot, wet tongue glide across her skin. Closing her eyes, she moaned, his thoughts racing amidst her own. After a few moments, she pulled her arm away and caressed the side of his face. She looked down at him for a moment before gently kissing his lips. His eyes were closed, his breathing shallow.

"Sleep now. You need to rest," she whispered.

CHAPTER 37

Alexis dressed quickly and grabbed Josh's gym keys. If memory served, she had a day to get everything prepped and ready for Josh when he woke up, *hungry*. Timing was everything.

Alexis made quick time from the gym to her house for supplies, but as she approached her house, she knew something was off. Pausing just around the corner, she watched and listened, picking up the different scents in the air. She didn't expect too many people out at three thirty a.m., yet somebody was. It was dark inside the house, and there were only a few of her personal belongings upstairs. Everything else was already on its way to her new destination.

She unlocked the door, stepping inside quickly before closing the door behind her. She didn't need light to tell her she had guests, humans. She could feel at least three different heartbeats. She scanned the space as she moved through the living room to the kitchen. She opened the refrigerator door, removing the remaining containers of blood. Setting them on the countertop, she heard the click of the light switch on the range hood.

Alexis couldn't help but smile, speaking before she turned around. "I believe this is breaking and entering." She saw their reflections in the window above the sink before she turned to face them. Two men and a woman standing around the kitchen, all dressed in black. *How mysterious.*

"You don't seem to live here anymore, so it's not *really* breaking and entering, is it?" the woman asked.

"It's mine until it sells and I turn over the keys," Alexis stated plainly. "What do you want?" She stared them down. She had no reason to show these people any respect after they made the decision to be done with her. *Damn coven.*

"We understand you *sired* another," the taller man stated.

Alexis rolled her eyes. *Good news sure does travel fast.* "That's right," she said. "He helped me take out Nika, since she killed Sebastian." She paused, looking away. "She killed him right in front of me, and there was nothing I could do."

"True as that may be, we just want to be sure you're not going to make it a habit of *perpetuating* your numbers," the woman said with a stern tone. "You understand our concern?"

Alexis's temper began to flare. She closed her eyes for a moment, regaining her control. She was getting better at it. Faster.

"You people are unbelievable," she declared. "I have lost *everybody* who has ever mattered to me, and you're worried about me increasing the numbers? The coven wants nothing to do with me now. I needed somebody I could trust, so I made an ally."

"We understand you are upset," the taller man said.

"*Upset?*" Alexis repeated the word, humored by the level of misunderstanding they had of her situation. "I'm going to make this really easy for you. You turned your back on me, which means what I do from now on is none of your damn business."

"On the contrary," the woman began. "Everything you do will continue to be a concern of ours. You were our last hope. You were to be stronger than anybody before you, and now . . ."

"What happened to me was not my fault," Alexis said, taking a step forward, a low growl escaping her lips. The members of the coven all took a step back, the stench of their fear filling the air. "If you're concerned about the other members of the coven, you shouldn't be. I have no intentions of hurting them as long as they don't try to hurt me." She scanned their faces.

"How do we know you're telling us the truth?" the woman asked, trying to stare Alexis down.

Alexis smiled, her teeth and eyes shifting, their fear increasing. "Well, I guess you're just going to have to trust me." Alexis was enjoying herself, perhaps a little too much.

"What about Lorcan McCowan?" the taller man asked.

"I would tell you not to worry about him, but he *is* still a threat, for now," Alexis stated.

"What do you mean?" the woman asked.

"What I mean is I'm leaving town. I doubt he is," Alexis said. "I need to regroup."

"The one you sired," the shorter man began. "Will he be leaving with you?"

"I can't imagine he will be staying since Lorcan probably wants him dead after killing Nika," Alexis announced. "He will not be traveling with me."

"Fine," the taller man replied. "Please do not contact any other members of the coven in the future, especially the remaining members of the Kincaid family. They are having a difficult time dealing with this already."

Alexis couldn't believe her ears. *What a bastard.* She shook her head and smiled. "No problem. Now, if we're done here, please get the hell out of my house."

The coven members looked at each other before walking out of the house. Alexis couldn't believe the coven felt they needed to send somebody to check up on her and her intentions. Looking around the kitchen, she found an empty box large enough to hold the containers of blood.

Alexis walked back into the living room, pausing to look around. So much had happened since she moved in all those years ago, and so much more had happened to her in the past few months. The living room looked different. It felt different. The happy memories of the past seemed to be slipping further away from her. She walked to the door, grasping the doorknob as she turned to look back one last time.

"Time for a new family to start some memories," she said out loud. She stepped outside and locked the door. The sun would be up in a few hours. In the meantime, she needed to get back to the gym and locked away with Josh. He had a small refrigerator to keep the blood fresh, and she needed to be there for him.

CHAPTER 38

Alexis entered the gym just after five a.m., locking the door behind her. She headed back to the private room behind the office where Josh was still sleeping. She studied him for a moment. He looked so peaceful, and she imagined that was how she looked when Sebastian found her. She walked over to the small refrigerator and put the containers of blood inside. She noticed the suitcases Josh had packed a few days earlier sitting in the corner of the room.

She sat down on the side of the bed for a minute before leaning back and curling up next to him. There was a comfort she felt with him now that wasn't there before. The connection with him was different than the one she'd had with Sebastian. Her love for Sebastian had been what dreams were made of. She cared for Josh, but it was not the same. Still, it felt nice to be close to someone again. As she drifted off to sleep, she wondered what her future held.

Alexis woke up around five p.m., happy to see Josh was still out. She got up and walked over to the refrigerator, retrieving a container of blood. She drained it quickly and stepped into the bathroom to rinse it out. From the bathroom, she heard Josh stir. Stepping back into the bedroom, she grabbed another container from the refrigerator and stood at the end of the bed, waiting for his eyes to open.

"Josh?" she whispered. "Can you hear me?"

His eyes opened slowly, and he stared up at the ceiling for a moment. He sat straight up in bed, his translucent blue eyes wide, a hungry look on his face. Alexis stepped closer, slowly placing one knee at a time on the bed. She sat back on her heels and studied him for a moment.

"Josh, I have what you need right here." She held the container close to her body, waiting for his reaction.

His eyes became fixed on it, and she knew the smell of the blood was driving him crazy. He reached forward slowly, and she handed the container to him. He quickly removed the lid and drank like he was starving.

"Slow down a bit. You need to let your system acknowledge what's happening." She stood up and backed away from the bed, watching him.

His eyes changed quickly back to their regular color of blue as he licked his lips clean. "Damn!"

"Are you okay?" she asked.

"I'm good," he replied. "I feel . . . *good*." He started smiling as he looked around the room. "I need a shower." He pulled the covers back and stood up, not bothered by the fact that he was naked. Alexis watched as he walked towards the bathroom. He *really* was quite spectacular. He paused in the doorway to look at her. "Wanna join me?" he asked, a naughty smile on his face.

Alexis laughed. "No, I'm okay." She sat back down at the end of the bed. She heard the water in the shower and waited patiently for him to return.

Twenty minutes later, he appeared with a towel wrapped around his waist. "Sorry about earlier."

"What do you mean?" she asked.

"My lack of modesty," he replied with a smile.

She stared at him for a moment. "*Are* you?" she finally asked, already knowing the answer.

His smile broadened, and she knew he was not. Looked like becoming a vampire was going to heighten his level of arrogance a bit. *This should be entertaining.* Still sitting on the edge of the bed, she watched as he dressed, surprised by how much control he already seemed to have. Probably due to all his training, or maybe it was just who he would always be.

"I know we should probably lay low for the next twenty-four hours until we head to the airport, but I'm not really sure that is the wisest choice." He finished dressing.

Alexis laughed out loud, shaking her head. "Josh, I know you want to go out and *play*, but we need to make sure Aidan doesn't locate either one of us."

"I agree, but don't you think I should find out how much control I have over my hunger pangs before getting on an airplane?" he asked. "I just think 35,000 feet is a bit high to discover I really *can't* fly."

Alexis couldn't really argue too much with that kind of logic. "Where would you like to go?"

"Let's take a walk."

"Okay," she replied. "Just remember, we are testing your control and not your new abilities to kill. God knows you already know how to do that *better* than most."

"I have a better idea," he announced.

"What's that?"

"Let's kill Aidan," he stated.

"Are you serious?" She walked over to the dresser.

"It's going to be a few hours before sunset," he professed, ignoring her question. "We should be able to come up with a plan in that amount of time."

"You really think it's a good idea to go after Aidan now? You *just* became a vampire."

Josh walked across the room to his dresser, studying his reflection in the mirror before picking up a brush and running it through his wet hair. "It's simple," he began, turning to face her. "We go to the club and take him down in Nika's old office."

She couldn't believe what she was hearing, but the look in his eyes told her he was serious. "How?"

"You go to the club right when it opens and make your way upstairs. I doubt anyone will know who you are since the club was closed the last time you were there," he explained. "Go up the staircase off to the right, the one you would pass going to the dance floor."

"I remember." She reflected over the last few weeks. It was hard to imagine how much her life had changed.

"At the top of the stairs, continue down the long hall past the opening on the left that leads to the balcony. The office is located at the end, the last door on the right."

"How can you be sure Aidan will be in the office?"

"The end of the month is coming," he stated. "Since he is currently without an office manager to look over the books, I *know* Aidan will be there."

"What do you want me to do exactly?" She felt like she was getting instructions for a covert operation. Then again, that *was* Josh's background.

"I want you to enter the office and start a conversation with him," he instructed.

"What should I wear?"

“Black, head to toe, and pull your hair back,” Josh replied. “Make sure you can move freely. Wear your heavy black leather boots and your black leather jacket. The material will offer you a little protection.” He studied her face for a moment. “It’s going to take both of us to take him down.”

“I know,” she whispered. “Where are you going to be?”

“I will be close by,” Josh replied with a grin. “Don’t worry,” he said reassuringly. “Oh, and don’t forget your gloves.”

CHAPTER 39

Part of this nightmare was finally going to end. If only everything could have been that easy. Alexis arrived at the club just as the last bit of light faded from the sky. She adjusted her gloves before reaching for the doorknob. Who knew a popular brand of glove would be used for such a nefarious design? She entered through the door from the alley, the same one she used before. Once inside, she paused, listening to the surroundings. The music was already blasting, and people were everywhere. She was thankful no one seemed to notice her.

There was a lot of security around, and she wondered if there was going to be a high body count to pull this off. It wasn't really what she was looking for, but she would do whatever was necessary to rid the world of Aidan Drake, and she knew Josh felt the same way.

Alexis waited until the hallway cleared before racing up the stairs. She paused at the top, looking around to make sure the coast was clear before moving quickly down the long hallway.

She stopped outside the office door. There was a little movement inside. She and Josh had not exactly synchronized their watches, but she trusted Josh to be there to back her up.

Alexis knocked on the door, entering the office before hearing an invitation. Aidan was sitting behind the desk across the room, a smile on his face.

"I was wondering when you would show up." He appeared relaxed, smug as a matter of fact. "How are you?"

"This isn't a social call," she replied, closing the door behind her and locking it. She glanced around the room, taking everything in. She watched Aidan carefully as she walked towards the desk, stopping just in front of the sofa, across from him. There was a window to her left covered in heavy drapes. She knew the drapes were new since Nika had been wrapped and burned in the old ones.

Aidan set the pen down in the binding of the large book in front of him. He leaned back in his chair, studying Alexis, the self-assured smile on his face only fueling the hatred she felt towards him.

"I know what you're feeling, my dear," he said.

"Somehow I *seriously* doubt that," she replied.

"You should really embrace your new life and all of its possibilities. In fact, the one who sired me imparted the same wisdom many years ago. Plus, in *their* eyes, you are less of a threat now."

"Whose eyes?" she asked. "Who are you referring to?" He was playing games with her. Maybe there was something to what he was saying, but then again, maybe there wasn't.

Aidan smiled, amused by her confusion. "So many opportunities and experiences await you. Carpe diem."

Alexis shook her head and smiled. "Actually, I have embraced a few opportunities recently."

"Have you now?" he asked, appearing genuinely curious.

"As a matter of fact, I have. I'm really taking control of my life lately . . . taking care of things and people who *interfere* with my business. People like Mr. Blake."

The smile widened across Aidan's face. "He was merely a pawn, an instrument to do my bidding," he stated. "He was actually quite easy to manipulate due to his *family* and *desperate* need for money." He shifted forward in his chair, leaning on the desk in front of him. Alexis stood her ground.

"That issue has been resolved," she stated. "I killed him."

"Did you enjoy killing him?"

"I did," she replied with a smile. "But I think I'm going to enjoy killing you more."

Aidan sat back in his chair, laughing, the sound resonating off the walls throughout the office. His reaction amused her. Aidan really *did* think he was untouchable.

Suddenly, he was on his feet, moving around the side of the desk towards her. He lunged, and she managed to evade his reach, instead catching him in the stomach with a solid roundhouse kick. He doubled over as she stepped away from him, spinning around to face him. She continued watching him carefully, wondering when Josh would make his entrance. Aidan looked at her again, his face twisted in anger.

"Do you really believe you can kill me, little girl?" His voice was steadier than Alexis expected. "We're just getting started."

Alexis started to move when the back of his left hand contacted the left side of her face, sending her crashing to the floor, blood trickling from a split in her bottom lip. She hadn't even seen him move, and when she started to look up, she felt his hand grip the back of her neck and pull her up off the floor. Her mind raced, and she wondered how she was going to get away from him. He pulled her close to his body, the fingertips of his left hand digging into her throat, as he pressed his mouth against her right ear from behind.

"You cannot beat me," his voice hissed. "You are as I *intended* you to be. Alone!"

Suddenly Josh burst through the window, rolling across the floor and onto his feet. His eyes locked on Aidan, ready to kill. Josh could tell Alexis was in a considerable amount of discomfort, the skin on her throat already bathed in color, her lip bleeding.

"Who the hell are you?" Aidan demanded, still holding her by the throat.

Josh smiled. "An ally."

Aidan's expression changed. He couldn't smell any humanity on the newcomer. "I see you *have* been busy, my dear," he stated mockingly. "You made a little friend."

Josh maintained his distance, but he knew they needed to finish this. Alexis wasn't looking too good.

"Do you really think the two of you can beat me?" Aidan's self-importance was going to be his downfall.

"You really are an arrogant bastard, aren't you?" Josh asked, grinning.

The expression on Aidan's face turned to irritation. Josh gave a nod, and Alexis elbowed Aidan in the solar plexus as hard as she could, causing the grip around her neck to fail. She threw her weight forward, executing a shoulder roll away from Aidan, towards the library table behind the sofa. Coming out of the roll, she reached out, breaking one of the legs off the table, then pivoted around but remaining in a crouched position. She watched Josh step forward and catch Aidan square in the jaw with a right hook followed by a roundhouse kick to the outside of his right leg just above the knee, dropping him to the floor. Aidan grunted in pain. Josh maneuvered behind him. Aidan rose on his knees, and Josh put him in a full nelson. Alexis executed another shoulder roll towards Aidan, driving the broken table leg into his heart. Josh retrieved his long, serrated blade from his boot, grabbed a handful of Aidan's hair and cut his head off in a single stroke.

They both stepped back and watched the body fall forward in a heap on the floor. Josh tossed the head down next to it.

"You okay?" he asked her, looking at her neck, bruises already forming. Her lip was still bleeding a bit as well.

"I'm good," she replied, staring down at the body. "Aside from the whole vise grip on my throat and a split lip, that was easier than I thought it would be. What took you so long?"

"I had some company in the alley."

"Spoils of war?" she asked, smiling at him.

"No," he replied with a laugh, admiring her darker side. "I only knocked them out."

Josh walked towards the window to pull the heavy drapes down to wrap around the body and the head. He seemed so calm, like this was an everyday occurrence. Of course, he *had* done this before.

"We aren't done yet," he announced, moving quickly to wrap up the body completely. "Now comes the hard part."

"What do you need me to do?" She stepped forward to help him.

"Get the body down to the incinerator in the basement and get out of here."

"What's your plan?"

"There's a door across the hallway leading down to the basement," he explained. "I need you to take care of anybody who gets in our way." He picked up the body and threw it over his shoulder.

"I can do that," she stated with a smile.

"Good job," he said, smiling proudly. "I've taught you well."

"Yes, you have. Is it heavy?"

"Just cumbersome, like deadweight can be," he replied dryly.

Alexis shook her head. "Funny."

"I try. Let's move."

Josh followed Alexis over to the door of the office. She unlocked it, opening it slowly to peer down the hallway. "Clear." She stepped into the hall, moving quickly off to the left and allowing Josh to get a head start to the basement door. He entered the hallway just as security was coming up the stairs.

"Hey!" the man yelled, running down the hall towards them.

"Go!" Alexis urged Josh. "I've got this."

Josh stepped through the doorway moments before the man from security reached Alexis. He tried to grab her by the arm and was met with a right palm heel strike to the solar plexus. He fell to the floor, gasping for air. Alexis turned, stepping through the doorway and closing the door behind her. She raced down the stairs in time to see Josh tossing the body into the incinerator. He closed the doors and hit the button, turning to look at her.

"We *really* need to go," she proclaimed.

"We're out," he replied.

Exiting the building, they paused on the stairs leading up to the street level in a crouched position, listening for a moment. So far, everything was quiet, but they both knew that would change once the security guy regained his composure. People were going to be looking for them.

"We need to get back to the gym and off the street," Josh declared.

"Lead the way."

They took off running and didn't stop until they reached the gym.

CHAPTER 40

"This is the final boarding call for flight 619 to New York," a voice announced over the intercom.

"That's me," Alexis stated. They stared at each other for a moment, unsure of what to say.

"Just remember, if you need to contact me, send it to the address I gave you," Josh said. "Dave will be our contact, and I know he can be trusted."

"I will. Thanks again, Josh, for everything." She stepped forward, gently brushing his lips with hers. She pulled back and stared into his eyes for a moment. She would miss him, but they both needed time and distance to discover who they were now.

He smiled at her. "Well, my gate is this way." He motioned in the opposite direction. "Take care of yourself, Alexis."

"I will. You too, Josh."

Alexis spun around, walking quickly towards the gate. She still hated good-byes. She also hated the fact that they had to kill

Aidan before he told her who *they* were. Now, she may never know.

Handing her boarding pass to the attendant, she thought about everything she needed to take care of when she reached her new home and, of course, all the things she'd always wanted to see. She would be in New York shortly and then her new home in three hours, by way of the Concorde. *Ah, the wonders of modern technology . . .*

EPILOGUE

Sitting down in his chair, Detective Mitchell began sifting through the newest folder waiting for him in his IN box. Too many unsolved murders lately and no new leads made for a grumpy captain.

"Hey, boss, we got another one," Ramirez called out from across the room.

"Let me guess," Mitchell began, "that big fancy nightclub downtown?"

"Good guess, boss."

Mitchell stood, grabbing his keys from his pocket. That place was turning into a real hot spot. Maybe this one would get closed, officially.

ACKNOWLEDGMENTS

Thank you to all the friends and family who have supported me throughout the process of this book, and to all the fuzzy creatures who inspired such colorful characters. You will be forever immortalized, as it should be.

Mom, thank you for listening to all the crazy ideas in my head, and for riding that creative roller coaster with me.

ELIZABETH ANNE GREY was born in Dallas, Texas, and grew up in Seattle, Washington. She has enjoyed writing throughout her life but her affinity for vampires goes back to childhood. Whether it was through movies or books, she always enjoyed the variations of vampire mythology.

She loves researching innovative ideas and information to include in her storytelling, and she utilizes the knowledge she gained studying interior design in college, as well as her life experiences working in the artwork and home improvement fields.

When she's not writing, Elizabeth enjoys action movies and comedies.

www.ingramcontent.com/pod-product-compliance
Lightning Source LLC
LaVergne TN
LVHW091635100826
845152LV00002B/41
9781737836506